PROJECT GENESIS

The Genesis Paradox

E.D. Moore

Pomenishi Publishing

pomenishi

CONTENTS

CHAPTER 1

The Genesis of Ambition

She could not believe what was happening. MJ lay sprawled across the cold, hard floor, her chest rising and falling in shallow, ragged breaths. Her fingertips brushed the pool of crimson blood that slowly spread beneath her—warm against the chill of the room. The gunshot had come so quickly, so suddenly that she had not fully processed it yet—the sharp crack of the bullet still echoing in her mind. As she came to grips with what had happened, she thought to herself, *"How did it come to this?"*

MJ was born in a sleepy, small town in Michigan, where the small roads seemed to stretch endlessly under a gray sky. Her hometown, a nondescript speck on the map, exuded a stifling quiet, the kind that settled into the bones like a nagging disease. As the boring town and its boring residents shuffled to and from their boring daily tasks, the drone of routine hung in the air, casting long shadows over any whispers of ambition.

MJ often felt suffocated by the sterile predictability surrounding her. Having descended from a line of accountants, actuaries and other mundane professionals did not help. She was trapped in a world built on a solid but utterly uninspiring foundation. She needed to escape.

MJ's desperation to be freed from her surroundings

reached an inflection point in her teens. It was as though she had suddenly awakened to the suffocating sameness that had always been there. The silent streets, the pointless local news stories, the predictable faces—it all was too small, too finite. No one cared that Ms. Peggy Sue had been selected by the township to organize the Patriot Day celebration or that Joe John took first place again in the local 5k race.

MJ would often lie awake at night, staring out the window at the night sky, dreaming of escaping. She dreamt of being a famous celebrity, signing autographs as paparazzi snapped photos of her wearing the latest fashion trends. She dreamt of winning the Nobel Prize, her portrait gracing the covers of science magazines. She dreamt of being the President of the United States, bringing an end to war and world hunger. She dreamt.

MJ's burgeoning awareness ignited a deep, restless curiosity within her, a hunger for something beyond her hometown's narrow confines and narrow minds. Her desire for more, however, was not appreciated by her family. Instead, her wishes became a sparking point for seemingly never-ending conflict with her parents during her hormone-fueled teens.

"No headphones at the table, dear," MJ's mother said as MJ began sitting down for dinner one evening.

"She can't hear you," MJ's father replied. "Her music is too loud, as usual."

"MJ," her mother repeated as she waved, trying in vain to get MJ to look up from her tablet. "MJ!" her mother repeated, struggling to raise her soft voice.

"MJ!" the father yelled as he snatched the headphones from MJ's ears, leaving a slight stinging feeling on her earlobes. "Your mother has been calling you, but of course you couldn't hear her with this god awful music blasting your eardrums to death!" he continued.

"God awful?" MJ asked rhetorically as she looked up at her father. She noticed his face was red with anger, but she did not care. "Isn't that blasphemy?" she asked sarcastically.

"No," her father replied as he sat back at the dinner table, still angry. "God would literally find that music to be awful."

MJ and her mother shared a quick glance. Her mother shook her head as if so tell MJ to let it go. MJ, however, could not control herself. "Really?" MJ responded, her tone condescending. "Did your magic sky daddy tell you that directly or through silent voices that only you can hear?"

Appalled, her father turned and looked at her mother. "Hunny, I'm getting really tired of dealing with this little girl's antics," her father said. "You better control her before I do," he added, shaking his head in disbelief.

"Let's all," the mother began before MJ interrupted.

"Well, you won't have to worry about dealing with me for much longer," MJ said. "I can't wait to graduate next year and get the heck out of this garbage town with all of you garbage small town yokels!"

"Now that is completely uncalled for, young lady," MJ's mother replied, her finger wagging in the air in disapproval.

"I'm not sure who you think you're talking to," MJ's father said. "A yokel is uneducated, and the only person without a college degree at this table is you, MJ."

"Relax, little fella," MJ responded. "You're just an accountant. Not a lot of world-changing mental gymnastics going on in your head."

MJ's mother put her hands on her face in utter disappointment.

"If you were smart, you would go to college here to get in-state tuition, become an accountant, and take over my clients," MJ's father replied smugly. "But, we all know you're not smart."

"Henry!" MJ's mother exclaimed.

"It's okay, mom. I'm used to people not believing in me," MJ said as she pushed aside her cabbage casserole, slowly stood, and began walking toward her bedroom.

Her father's words cut deep into MJ's psyche. With her door locked, she silently cried herself to sleep. She did not dream about being famous or winning the Nobel Prize that evening. She simply dreamt of proving her father wrong as he aged into oblivion.

Her father's words stung the most because, deep down, MJ knew she had failed to demonstrate her intellectual promise. She had no response because she knew she could not refute what he was saying. In fact, MJ had shown herself to be a barely above-average person in nearly every way imaginable.

She was intelligent but did not have the grades to match. She was pretty enough but not remarkably so. She was neither lame nor popular, athletic nor uncoordinated. She was just there, occupying space but not making a lasting mark.

However, despite her mere above-average nature, MJ knew that her mind, abilities, and goals were too expansive for her surroundings. She felt trapped, caught between the mundane expectations of her environment and the unproven potential she was confident existed within her.

By her senior year of high school, MJ's restlessness had transformed into resolve. She promised herself to leave behind her town and attend college far away—somewhere "relevant" with "relevant people" like her. That plan did not go as she hoped.

MJ was systematically rejected from every single prestigious university to which she applied. She was devastated, her confidence shaken as she faced major rejection from the outside world for the first time. MJ, however, was not a quitter. She re-took her admissions exam at the beginning of her final semester, determined to improve her prospects.

Ultimately, she was accepted into a university on the islands of Los Angeles. It was not Ivy League, but she felt the university, somewhat prestigious yet approachable, was well matched to her ambitions. Moreover, it was ranked higher than the schools her friends had decided to attend.

MJ's parents initially balked at the idea of her moving to California, not just because it meant leaving the safety of their town but out of fear of further natural disasters that had turned Southern California into a series of disconnected islands. Eventually, however, both parents grew to be happy for MJ and to respect her decision. Still, there was always some tension between MJ and her father, but they both burried it inside.

As her departure day drew closer, MJ found herself standing on the edge of the town's lookout point. The view was not much, but it was home. She wondered if she was being selfish for wanting more; if she was turning her back on something that was not so bad after all. "*Was dad right all along?*" she asked herself. "*Am I giving up a sure thing for dreams that will never come to fruition?*" "*Am I making a smart decision?*" "*Am I an indiot and I'm the only one who can't see it?*"

MJ though deeply about cancelling her trip, withdrawing her enrollment, and staying home. Then, the thought of her father challenging her intelligence flooded her mind. Her face began to turn red as anger bubbled up inside her. She needed to prove him wrong. She needed to prove to the world, to everyone who doubted her, to her friends, family, and the universities that rejected her, that she was born to be great.

MJ arrived at her university intent on building a new, more exciting life that matched her greatness—a simultaneous quest for new horizons and an escape from mediocrity. There, amidst sunny skies and bright minds, her path took an unexpected turn when she met George—an encounter that would forever change MJ and the world.

MJ met George on a sweltering afternoon as she wandered across the sprawling campus. Lost in her thoughts and her map as she meandered, MJ collided with a tall young man. He was soft-spoken, with an awkward smile, his eyes hidden behind thick-rimmed glasses that reflected the extreme midday sun.

"Excuse me," MJ said, brushing her hair out of her face. "I'm so sorry."

"No, excuse me," George replied, a slight tremble in his voice as he timidly smiled at MJ.

"Hey, do you know where the student health services building is?" MJ replied.

George glanced at her again, his face flushing slightly. "It's just up ahead," George pointed, offering a smile that didn't quite reach his eyes. "I can show you."

"You sure? I don't want to drag you off course." She shifted her gaze to the ground, half-expecting him to brush her off like so many others had.

George hesitated, then nodded. "I've got time. Besides, it's better than wandering around campus alone." His voice wavered as if unsure of himself, but there was a flicker of something more. Pride? Confidence? MJ couldn't tell.

"So, are you a freshman," the young man asked, his voice steadying.

"Yep," she replied. After an awkward silence, she added, "I have to take care of some vaccination things or whatever. Can't be responsible for a rabbit pox outbreak or whatever this year's pandemic will be. I'm MJ, by the way."

"Hi, MJ. I'm George, but my friends call me... George, I guess," he replied while chuckling.

MJ politely chuckled in response, though she did not understand the joke.

"Yeah, so we're here," George stated as he placed his finger at a specific point on the map. "And you need to get to there," George directed MJ further on the map.

A look of confusion crept across MJ's face.

"Here, how about I walk you," he offered.

"If it's not too much trouble. Thank you... truly!" MJ replied.

As the two walked, they conversed briefly about where they were from, what they were studying, and which professors they had.

"Well, it looks like we are here," George stated.

"Thanks again!" MJ replied.

"No worries. See you around!" George started walking away, awkwardly turned, and yelled, "Hey, MJ! Some of us are getting together later if you wanna. Just hit me on my Pomen. My username is Georgeous1, George O U S the number one!"

MJ giggled. "Sure thing! Will do!"

George and MJ grew closer over her first semester at the university. George was two years ahead of MJ and had selected Computer Engineering as his major. MJ declared her major at the end of her first year. Whether out of a subconscious desire to be closer to George, an emerging passion for coding, or divine intervention to bring about the events to come, MJ declared Computer Engineering as her major with a minor in General Business—Marketing. George congratulated MJ on her choice, though MJ could not shake the feeling that George was somewhat irritated that she was following in his footsteps.

No matter the reason she selected her major, Computer Engineering challenged and fascinated MJ equally. It was also a realm where she came to a stark realization–the intellectual giants around her were a far cry from the competition she had barely outpaced in her hometown. The realization had hit her like a ton of bricks on day one when she discovered that each of her classmates had already been coding for years. While she had been daydreaming during her teens, her classmates, like her new friend Janina, had taught themselves to code. She was far behind.

Fueled by her desire to prove herself and to avoid embarassment, MJ persisted, undeterred and intent on rising to the challenge. Rather than go to house parties, she spent extra time in the computer lab. Instead of tailgating at football games, she read computer science books and online forums recommended by Janina and George. She was slowly catching up.

"I aced the algorithms exam!" MJ exclaimed to George as she burst into his dorm room one morning, with a look of pure excitement plastered across her face. "I might be one of the top students in class!" she continued.

"Great job, very cool," George replied in a monotonous tone as he barely looked up from his work, forcing a smile.

"Man, I guess hard work really does pay off," MJ added.

"That's great, but I'm a little busy," George replied.

"For sure. And thanks for the help. I guess I needed it more than I realized." Sensing something off, MJ scanned George's face for a reaction.

George shrugged, avoiding her gaze. "It's no big deal. I've been doing this for a while."

"Yeah, well... let's hope I can keep up." The words hung in the air between them. "Okay, well...you seem busy, so I'll take off and check in with you later," MJ replied, her joyful mood ruined.

"Bye," George replied as he waved his hand at MJ dismissively, his head still buried in the textbook.

Despite the occasional tension and subtle signs of annoyance and jealousy in their relationship, MJ and George continued dating throughout college. Even after graduating two years before MJ, George continued helping MJ. Still, MJ could not shake the feeling that something about their relationship was strange. Something about George was strange.

When George graduated a couple of years before MJ, he secured an entry-level position at tech giant Pomenishi Technology (known globally as "PomenTech"), where he had interned the previous summer. MJ had visited him once in Chicago during that summer to escape her town during her summer back home. It was just a few hours' drive. During her visit, MJ attempted to attend various social events hosted by PomenTech. She asked George multiple times if she could join him, explaining that it could be a good networking experience for her to build inroads at the company. George, however, always had an excuse as to why she could not attend PomenTech social events with him. He explained how confidentiality concerns prevented her from being allowed in the highly secure facility. He explained how no one brought significant others to co-worker happy hours. He explained how he and his work friends were so low-level that it would be useless to network with them. George always had an excuse.

"Is he hiding something?" MJ asked herself. *"Does he not want me to work with him for some reason?" "Does he have another girlfriend at work?" "What's his deal?"*

Despite George's refusal to help, MJ applied for an internship with PomenTech. Her application was rejected and she was forced to intern with a small non-profit teaching children basic coding skills.

MJ spent the better part of her last semester applying for post-graduate entry-level computer programming jobs in Chicago. Like her initial college applications, every single company rejected her. Adding to her woes, her grades also slipped as she stopped seeking help from George out of an unspoken frustration she had developed with how he treated her.

She ultimately graduated in May with a 3.3 grade point average but was unemployed. Needing a place to live but not wanting to move back home and prove her father right, MJ asked George if she could move in with him. He agreed, though MJ had a nagging feeling that he did so reluctantly.

MJ remained unemployed until early August when she received an unexpected letter from PomenTech advising that they had reconsidered her application and were offering her a job on their software development team in light of the renewed market emphasis on technological innovation.

It was like a dark cloud had cleared from above MJ. She was over the moon with excitement at the offer and with the belief that George had turned the page and decided to help her behind the scenes.

"*Babe, guess what!*" she texted George.

"*Idk…what?!*" George responded with alacrity.

"*I think you already know, but PT just offered me a job as a junior developer!*"

"*I didn't know. Why do you think I knew?*"

"*They rejected me and now, out of nowhere, offer me the job… Smells like you pulled some strings or put in a good word!*"

"*Nope. I can't reach the strings, lol. With the Strategy Nine announcement, I know they're desperate to hire anyone with a pulse.*"

George's message was yet another jab at her value. She did not understand why he treated her so poorly. In hindsight, MJ should have recognized the signs of George's coming betrayal. She should have broken up with him immediately, saving millions of lives, George's included. In the moment, however, she just felt confused and did not respond to his text.

The tension that hovered over MJ and George's relationship only intensified after she joined PomenTech, once again following in George's shoes. MJ started as a Junior Developer, working on the same team as George, working on the same projects as George, interacting with the same colleagues and superiors as George, and attending the same meetings as George. He could not shake her from his shadow.

In meetings, MJ would generally be a background character. George would be more actively involved and relevant. Eager to be heard and seen at one meeting, however, MJ proposed a small new idea as an alternative to one of George's ideas. She received positive feedback from their superiors. George, however, was not pleased with his younger girlfriend having undermined him.

"That went well, don't you think?" MJ asked as she jogged and caught up to George as he headed back to his desk after the meeting ended.

"Yeah, great. Not everyone needs to stand in the spotlight, though," George responded.

"What do you mean?"

"If you disagreed with me, you could have brought it up with me later. You didn't have to embarass me in front of everyone."

"I didn't embarass you. We were just brainstorming."

"Don't gaslight me, MJ. You wanted to look smarter than me. It's sad, really."

"Wow. That's not what happened, but okay. I don't think I'm smarter than you."

"I didn't say you thought you were smarter than me. We all know you aren't," George said as he smugly chuckled, knowing the history with her father and that those words would hurt her most.

"Wow. You sound like my father. What a jerk! Why do you always have to demean my intelligence?"

"I'm not!" George exclaimed as people began looking at the couple. "It would just be nice if you found something of your own for once and stopped hanging on my coattails," George added as he tried to calm his tone to avoid making a scene.

"Coattails? Coattails! You know what!" MJ thought for a brief second about breaking up with George at that moment. "Let's just talk about this later," MJ added as she tried to calm herself.

MJ and George went their separate ways toward their desks mere feet apart. Later that evening, they both avoided the conversation.

As the months wore on, the tension began to grow between

MJ and George. George's support for MJ's accomplishments felt increasingly strained, his smiles forced, his congratulations half-hearted. George's confusion about his feelings for MJ's successes became increasingly more transparent. It was becoming noticeable to MJ that George wanted to support her but could not help but feel left out and unnoticed, overshadowed by someone he felt was never truly passionate about the work but instead just copying him. MJ could now see that, beneath the surface, a complex mixture of emotions simmered within George—pride and admiration, yes, but also something darker.

George had always been the golden child in his family—a straight-A student, the one everyone expected to rise to the top. His father, a software engineer himself, never let George forget that anything less than perfection was a failure. "You're destined for greatness," his father had said repeatedly to George, every word a weight George carried into adulthood. But George had begun to feel the cracks at the university and even more at PomenTech, surrounded by equally (if not more) ambitious minds.

George could not shake the feeling that, despite his beliefs about his greatness, he was just another cog in the corporate machine, struggling to stand out. MJ's growing success only sharpened the edges of his doubt—*was he as brilliant as he had been told, or had he been riding on praise all along? If a novice like MJ could achieve the same things as he could, was he even special?*

Every time MJ made progress, she could see a tightening in George's chest—she could empathically feel a nagging sense of inadequacy growing within him. He had always been the one to shine, but now, MJ was casting a shadow over him, one that seemed to grow with each new success she achieved. MJ had always believed she would surpass George but had neither predicted his insecurity nor what he would do in a fit of desperation to keep her from surpassing him.

CHAPTER 2

The Sands of Innovation

The Chairman sat there in the darkness. As his mind poured over all that happened that day, he suddenly lost control and burst into tears. *"How could I have been so naiive?"* he thought to himself. *"I left her vulnerable, exposed. And they took her away from me."*

The Founder and Chairman of the Board of Directors of PomenTech was a smart, tough, and admired man. Known most simply as the "Chairman," he was a mysterious figure. The world knew him for his genius that had introduced quantum machine learning, generalist A.I. agents, and truly immersive virtual reality. The world also knew him as a highly-competent and fearless leader and a staunch supporter of advancing A.I. technology. Beyond that, however, the Chairman was a mystery. And he like it that way.

"Good day, Welsley," the Chairman said to the robotic android that greeted him as he walked through the doors of PomenTech's headquarters, aptly named the Tower of Innovation. "Please give me today's headlines," he continued as the android followed along. "And please have breakfast prepared for me and Sophie, something savory and sweet today. Thank you."

"Certainly, sir," Welsley responded in a robotic tone. The Chairman had been adamant that androids look and sound like androids, not humans. To the chagrin of many, he was a dogged supporter of maintaining a seperate existence between humans and androids. "Humanity is fragile," he would preach to his Board of Directors. "We must keep our hubris in check and avoid overly mimicking ourselves, lest we confuse ourselves as to what it means to be human."

The lobby gleamed with almost sterile perfection as the Chairman continue his path through the building. The soft, cold illumination from massive overhead lights cast sharp reflections on the pristine marble floors. The Chairman's footsteps echoed from the floor to the forty-foot ceiling, over to the massive panoramic windows overlooking the city.

Executing the Chairman's command, Welsley caused a holographic news anchor to blink into existence. "Today is September twenty-first, two thousand sixty, and here are your morning's top headlines," it began.

"The markets have taken yet another plunge as the conglomerate, Pomenish Technology has released yet another quarterly earnings report in the red." The words echoed awkwardly. "In other news, Artificial intelligence activist organization, AIA, has organized yet another nationwide protest, seeking adoption of an A.I. Bill of Rights," the anchor continued. "The protest ended in violence as chaos ensued shortly after two rival factions within AIA began heatedly debating whether A.I. should be treated the same as humans or given separate but equal treatment. The division led to pushing and shoving that evolved into an all-out brawl."

"In other news," the anchor continued. "In stark contrast to the Great Disconnect of years past, the United States government has launched a new directive to restore the U.S. to the forefront of innovation. As the world learned when disconnecting from technology became a, short-lived, but impactful, trend, they who lead innovation, lead the world.

Since the Great Disconnect began, that leader has been China. The federal government is now launching its Strategy Nine initiative to restore the U.S. to the forefront."

"What is our progress on Strategy Nine?" the Chairman asked his android as they continued walking toward his executive elevator.

"Sir, Pomenishi Technology's 10-year, five hundred billion dollar federal grant agreement under Strategy Nine has been fully signed," Welsely responded.

"Excellent. What's the next step?"

"Today, we expect to receive security clearances from the National Security Agency. Once those clearance are received, we expect to receive a meeting invitation from the U.S. President's Joint Chiefs of Staff to discuss both the consumer and top secret military aspects of the Strategy Nine grant."

"Excellent. Thank you, Welsley," the Chairman responded with excitement as he and the android entered the executive elevator. As the elevator door began to close, however, two hands reached in and pulled the doors open. Two towering men in black suits and sunglasses displayed badges to the Chairman and directed him to follow them immediately. The Chairman, startled by the abruptness, complied.

The Chairman, having been whisked away in an all black air taxi, arrived quickly at the Pentagon in Washington D.C. As he exited the taxi at the front of the facility, he paused for a moment, enamored and somewhat intimidated by the massive, majestic walls in front of him.

"This way, sir," one of the men directed him.

"Certainly," the Chairman replied. "Who am I meeting with, the Joint Chiefs?"

"I'm not privy to that information, sir. Just follow me."

The agents walked the Chairman through the initial set of thick metal doors, but they were not allowed any further.

After a facial scan and fingerprinting, a military officer directed the Chairman to follow the LED arrows on the floor to his destination. As the lights embedded in the thick concrete floor began to pulse and flow, the Chairman began following the illuminated path. The path led him through a series of maze-like halls, onto an elevator, and to a set of massive double-doors.

A gentle, rising harmonic tone began to emanate from the door, like the hum of a digital device coming to life. A series of blue light rays began scanning the Chairman's body. The door then emitted a sharp chime, followed by a series of clanks and the sound of gears turning. The doors opened and the Chairman entered the dark room.

The room was grand in size, with a large round table at the center. Seated around the table in tall-backed, sturdy-built leather chairs were a series of government officials. There were no nametags or nameplates, just a group of serious-looking individuals spread around the table with spotlights beaming down on each individual. There was one seat open. The Chairman took it.

"Good morning, all. Let's get to the point," a gruff gentleman in military regalia began as the others stopped their side conversations and gave him their full attention. "Mr. Chairman, we've called you here to make sure you understand the military directives applicable to your company under Strategy Nine."

"Thank you for having me," the Chairman began before he was interrupted by the gentleman.

"Pomenishi Technology's directive is to develop advanced machine-learning algorithms and tools for war simulation. These algorithms and tools are to include social unrest prediction models, foreign leader decisionmaking prediction models, and other tools useful for war simulation."

"Understood, sir," the Chairman began before he was again interrupted by the gentleman.

"We expect that Pomenishi Technology will accomplish this, in substantial part, through neural mapping of the world population with a particular emphasis on mapping the minds of foreign government leaders through their use activity on Pomenishi Technology applications. Do you understand, Mr. Chairman?"

"Yes, I think I do. But, I have a few concerns about the neural mapping. We will need consent..."

"No consent is needed and under no circumstance will you inform anyone outside of this room of such neural mapping. Is that clear?"

"What about the legal..."

"Do not worry about any legal aspects. This is a national security directive, giving your company immunity with respect to all actions taken at our direction. I expect we are clear now. We will schedule periodic meetings to check on your progress. Thank you."

The Chairman had additional questions and concerns, but everyone rose from their seats and left the room. The Chairman was left sitting at the empty table, wondering what he had gotten himself into.

A native of Chicago's southside where PomenTech was headquartered, the Chairman was no stranger to dealing with tough individuals. Having successfully navigated gritty gang-infested streets and cutthroat corporate boardrooms, the Chairman was no pushover. The Strategy Nine directive, however, had taken him outside of his comfort zone and made him feel small.

As he returned to the solitude of his office that dominated the entire 55th floor of the Tower of Innovation, the Chairman stood before the vast expanse of glass, the city sprawled out beneath him like a living, breathing organism. As the sun's reflection from the skyscrapers shimmered in the distance, his mind was elsewhere—caught in a vortex of fear and ambition. His tall, dark, and handsome reflection in the window stared back at him, a silent reminder of everything at stake.

PomenTech's throne atop the technological world felt precarious, teetering on the edge of something unknown. Each success had been a stepping stone, but success had been difficult to come by in recent years. A few news reports hinted at the company's inability to turn a profit in recent months, but only the Chairman was fully aware of the dire situation facing the company. A company built on constant innovation, PomenTech's bank of novel ideas had dried up. The company needed the Strategy Nine grant, but the Chairman was simultaneously unsure whether they could produce the necessary results.

The Chairman's last groundbreaking innovation felt like a distant memory, and he had since relied heavily on his staff for new ideas. The "Innovation Team," as they were called, was a coveted group, a collection of the brightest minds handpicked by the Chairman himself. He ensured they were well-compensated to fend off competitors and had all the resources they needed to keep them happy and productive. Yet even their ideas had started to feel stale. The government grant was a blessing, but the Chairman knew it could quickly become a curse if he did not find a way to deliver.

Pacing around his office's sleek, almost monolithic grandeur, the Chairman thought to himself deeply. As he paced past the floor-to-ceiling windows that wrapped the space in a panorama of the city below and Lake Michigan beyond, he began to hum a song to himself. As the soft pulse of LED mood lighting created an ethereal glow against his white marble floors, the Chairman began to drift deeper into thought, deeper into his mood. His pace began more rhythmic, almost a dance, as holographic art shifted and flowed across the walls, their forms occasionally interrupted by physical sculptures displayed in sleek glass cases. Soon, he began to sing at the top of his lungs, dominating the entire space with his vocals. Just then, the idea struck him.

"An innovation competition!" he blurted out, the spark of an idea igniting in his eyes. "We'll open the Innovation Team to every single person in this company—a grand competition to reshape the future," he declared, a sly grin curling at the corners of his lips. His fingers interlaced, rubbing together like a mastermind plotting the next revolution as if the blueprint for something world-shattering had just crystallized in his mind.

"But, what drives people? What will motivate them to give it their best?" he mused aloud, his voice now barely more than a whisper. "*Money? Power? Prestige?*" he thought to himself. He needed something that would reignite the fire of invention within his team, something that could save PomenTech from stagnation and demise.

Little did the Chairman know, the seeds of a revolutionary idea were already being sown within the walls of PomenTech, an idea that would challenge the very foundations of reality and humanity.

CHAPTER 3

The Apocalypse of Ambition

MJ felt small in the vast expanse of the PomenTech lobby as she eagerly arrived for her first day of work. It felt like she was stepping into another world. The rigid security protocols, the cold futuristic atmosphere, the bustling groups of people and androids, it all made her feel like she was joining a massive, fast-moving train. Unlike George, however, she did not feel like she was just another cog in the global PomenTech machine. *"This is perfect,"* she thought to herself. *"This is where I will leave my mark. This is my platform."* She was correct, but had no idea the level of sacrifice it would take.

PomenTech was a veritable Fort Knox. As a part of the Strategy Nine grant, PomenTech was required to strengthen its security protocols to meet military-grade expectations. Every project, idea, and line of code at PomenTech was monitored, logged, and stored in encrypted databases. Access to sensitive projects was even more heavily restricted.

MJ, a Junior Developer, was rarely granted access to anything of material importance. Instead, she often found herself buried in endless lines of independently unimportant code, though she was sure her work was an important piece of something larger. While getting work done seemed to come with ease for some of her colleagues, MJ routinely had to stay at work for a few hours after others, desperate to impress —desperate to prove she belonged. It felt unfair, but MJ was determined not to give up. If anything, her early struggles pushed her harder to succeed.

In contrast, George had used his two-year head start to quickly navigate the corporate ladder with steady determination and general brilliance. Despite his insecurity and lack of self-confidence, George had progressed within the company at a pace far greater than his contemporaries, rising multiple rungs above MJ. George had both a drive to work hard and a natural brilliance. MJ secretly envied George for the latter.

As a more senior and trusted employee than MJ, George had greater access to PomenTech's systems and built better relationships with staff and Senior Developers. He thus had a greater glimpse into the inner workings of PomenTech and a better understanding of how to succeed. However, that heightened level of access, coupled with his unspoken disdain for MJ's successes, would soon unite and set George on a direct collision course with MJ.

"It feels like we're drifting," MJ abruptly stated to George one evening, almost under her breath as the two sat on opposite ends of the couch—the blue light from their immersive reality system reflecting off their skin. George had arrived home from a late night at the office a few minutes earlier, eclipsing MJ's already late night. "You're always at work, and when you're home, you're still not really here," MJ added with a bit more conviction in her voice.

George coldly replied, "What do you want me to do? It's not like I'm sitting around while you're off changing the world." George let out a chuckle saturated with condescension.

"What's that supposed to mean?" MJ inquired accusingly as she sat up firmly, her eyes glaring at him.

"Nothing. Just forget about it. Can I just decompress for a

moment?" George replied, his frustration filling the air.

"Why do you... why do you do this to me?" Her voice cracked, and she looked away, trying to steady herself. "I thought you... loved me, but all you do is tear me down."

George opened his mouth but said nothing, shifting uncomfortably.

MJ turned to face him again, her eyes narrowing. "What's the deal, George? Say something."

"I don't know what you're talking about," George replied.

"You're always downplaying my successes...really, anything I do. I get good grades and you give me half-hearted congratulations. I get a job at PomenTech and you tell me its because they'll hire anyone with a pulse. It almost like..."

"Like what," George replied.

"It's almost like you're jealous!" Saying the words felt like lifting a burden from her mind that had weighed her down for years.

"What! Me, jealous of *you*! You're basically a glorified tech support worker. Meanwhile, I have a million things on my plate that actually help the company move forward. I don't complain about that, but now you complain about me because my job is harder. It's not my fault."

MJ rose to her feet, her anger boiling over. "No one is forcing you to work day in and day out like a PomenTech slave! I mean...you volunteer for all of this. You're always the first one in the meeting to say, 'Sure, I can handle that...I can take a crack at it boss man.' And now you complain that your job is harder and I'm a glorified Tech Support worker." MJ's words hung in the air. "Why can't you be like everyone else and just do what is asked and then live your life, our life?" MJ added.

"Be like everyone else?" George questioned in a sarcastic tone. "Like you, an utter and complete..."

"An utter and complete what," MJ interrupted as George searched for the right words.

"An utter and complete follower! You have no independent passion of your own," George added.

MJ sat back down in silence, George's words echoing in her head like a piercing whistle, once again reminding her of her father.

"I didn't mean it like that," George replied, his tone now somber as he tried to backtrack from his statement. "I just meant, I want you to find what you're passionate about, what you love… and pursue that. It feels like you just do what I do, and I know that's not what you really want."

MJ rose from the couch slowly, her head tilted down, her eyes tearing up as she stared at the floor. "I'm just gonna go to bed," she replied in a defeated tone as she left the room.

George's words from their argument burned into MJ's brain like a cattle brand. MJ could not take her mind off of the argument—ruminating throughout the days and even more at night. "*He's not wrong,*" she often thought to herself. "*But he's not right.*"

MJ did not bother George with her thoughts or discuss the argument for days. George also seemed fine with ignoring the argument, though tension was undoubtedly in the air. Instead, MJ decided to press those emotions deep inside. But, depressed emotions have a funny way of bubbling to the surface.

One evening, as MJ and George tried to relax in their apartment, MJ found herself reminiscing about simpler times. Times when she did not worry about jobs, relationships, or impressing others. As she thought back on those childhood days, she could not help but smile.

"What's up? Why the giddy smile?" George asked as he scooted closer to MJ, reaching his arm around her shoulder and pulling her in for a cuddle.

"Do you ever miss the good ole days," MJ replied, looking into George's eyes—a look of longing deep within her. "Like… sitting on the back porch doing pretty much nothing?" MJ asked, her voice filled with a whispered joy.

"Um…maybe," George replied.

"Not like being on social media, but simpler. Playing card games, digging in the dirt, building bike ramps, just…being."

"I guess so. I never did that whole Great Disconnect thing though," George chuckled. "Not a lot of dirt digging in New York. And my parents were tech junkies and so was I."

"I guess you're right," MJ replied. "Obviously, my mom and dad are not big techies. If I spent too much time inside, they would kick my butt right out of the house and tell me to go find something to do," MJ said as she chuckled. "But, I had a loophole," she continued. "My parents were big into early 2000's tech. I think it made them feel good talking about their DVD collections, pulling out their old MP3 players, and reminiscing on 'simpler times.'"

"I don't know what any of that is," George replied as he laughed.

"They would let me play with some of the old tech they collected. My favorite was the NanoPets. I took that thing with me everywhere. Gotta be a good parent and whatnot." MJ chuckled at the thought.

"What's a NanoPet?" George asked, his tone both curious and amused.

"Seriously?" MJ quipped playfully. "Your parents never taught you about the classics?" MJ explained in almost loving detail, "A NanoPet was a digital pet you could carry around in your pocket or hang from your belt loops. You would take care of it like a real-life pet; feeding it and whatnot." MJ said, "Someone should bring it back—a NanoPet for modern times. With our new technology, the NanoPet would be frickin' amazing!"

Ever the pragmatist, George voiced doubts about the appeal of such an idea in a world saturated with advanced technology. Those doubts crept into MJ's mind as she reflected on his energy.

"I guess I'm not sure if my idea is good enough," MJ added later that night. "I mean, I've been thinking about it, but… I don't know if it can work." She bit her lip, glancing nervously at

George.

"I didn't know you were serious," George replied. "If you're serious about it, we can talk more and see if there is potential."

"Really!" MJ exclaimed, happy to have George's support. "Well, I'm thinking, with our technology, we could really bring this thing to life."

"What do you mean," George asked with a quizzical expression on his face.

"The NanoPet never really did much, but what if it was powered by A.I.?" MJ added as her eyes lit up.

George thought for a moment. "Hmmm...that could work. It could think and behave like a real life animal," George said.

"Yeah, and the graphics would be amazing. It would look real," MJ added.

"Heck, it could even live in the house with you...a holographic pet," George said as he began to match MJ's excitement. "No cleaning up poop, no destroying your furniture. And we could monetize by having people buy digital clothes and food for their pets!"

MJ's idea was the spark of passion and innovation she had been longing for. It was finally an original thought of hers that she could nurture into a flame. A flame that would ignite the world.

When the Chairman announced the innovation competition, MJ saw it as a sign that she should seriously pursue her NanoPet idea. She planned to submit it as her competition entry and, hopefully, develop it with the backing of PomenTech. This was her chance to prove her worth—not just to PomenTech or her father, but to herself. This would surely be her moment to shine —to build something that grew from her own passions.

MJ put her all into refining the concepts. She and George debated whether it should be a holographic pet or if they should shoot for the stars and try to create something more realistic. An android pet? No, that felt derivative and had failed many companies before. A real-life clone of a pet, biologically engineered to not poop, pee, and destroy? That seemed overly ambitious and outside of even PomenTech's abilities. Then, the idea hit her.

"What about miniature clones of pets?" MJ posited to George.

"Hmm...I like where you're going with this," George replied as he rubbed his chin in contemplation.

"They would be small enough that their messes and destructive behaviors would be negligible," MJ added.

"Okay. Okay. That could work," George added as he nodded his head. "But if they are tiny, wouldn't they get hurt or killed... like a lot?"

"Good point," MJ said as she mulled over the various problems.

"Maybe put them in like a fish tank or something," George added.

MJ nodded in silence, her mind clearly on to something big. "Yeah. Or even better, a tiny world of their own."

"Yeah, like a fish tank with everything they need," George replied.

"No. Bigger," MJ said as she spread her arms wide in demonstrative fashion. "Literally a world of their own, housed in a box. Grass, trees, rivers, other creatures. They could have it all!"

George thought for a moment. "That is freaking awesome!" George exclaimed before he let his pragmatic thoughts cloud his mind. "It sounds crazy complicated, though. I'm not sure we could make that work. Or if we could, it might cost so much that we would have to price it higher than any average consumer would pay."

Over the next few weeks, MJ continued mulling over and refining her idea. Between completing her daily PomenTech tasks, she would pull out her PomenTech-provided digital notebook and work on her NanoPet project. George and MJ began spending more time together too as he took a strong interest in helping with her project. All was going well. For some reason, however, MJ could not shake the feeling that something was off.

As MJ delved deeper into her project, her workload suddenly increased. She was assigned to multiple new projects, each high priority, making it impossible for her to focus on her competition entry. Overwhelmed, MJ tried to speak with the supervisor but was met with vague explanations about the company's needs. MJ reluctantly accepted the excuses, intent on maintaining, and hopefully improving, her reputation as a good employee. Her desire to please, however, had made her blind to the treachery that had befallen her.

Unbeknownst to MJ, through casual conversations and subtle favors, George had managed to learn about the workflow and project allocation system, which operated with high-level security and required multiple authentication steps for access. George did not hack the system directly—instead, he exploited his connections. By convincing a lower-level project manager that he was conducting a "workload audit" for a senior team member, George gained temporary access to the project scheduling tools.

Once inside the system, George made careful adjustments, adding MJ to high-priority projects that would monopolize her time without drawing attention to his actions. The changes were small and seemingly innocuous, blending in with the company's standard project loads, but they were enough to overwhelm her. Moreover, George knew better than to leave a direct trail, using the project manager's credentials, which were logged as part of a routine adjustment, masking his interference under the guise of normal operations.

As the competition deadline approached, MJ was buried under tasks, with almost no time for her competition entry. She failed, despite spending an ungodly amount of time trying to accomplish work and work on her competition entry. On the night before the deadline, she succumbed to the reality that she would not be able to finish her competition entry. She was angry with PomenTech for creating a roadblock that prevented her from taking advantage of her moment to see her dreams become reality. But she mostly felt frustration and disappointment in herself for failing and not having the resolve needed to prove her greatness.

The next day came and went. MJ missed the competition deadline, not submitting her idea in its incomplete state out of fear that it would be rejected as not good enough. She was devastated and lost.

Months later, the competition winner was announced in a company-wide meeting. The Chairman, ever the showman, performed a grandiose augmented reality reveal of the winner and a mock-up of the idea. PomenTech's employees gathered in the grand auditorium, unaware of the tensions brewing beneath the surface. As the final employee was seated, the lights went dim, and all focus was on the stage. After a brief introduction, the Chairman announced the winner.

"Without further ado, the winner of the Inaugural PomenTech Innovation Competition is... George Walker!" exclaimed the Chairman.

George, who had been informed of his victory earlier in the day, walked out onto the stage from behind the left curtain, smiling from ear to ear as he took his place next to the Chairman.

"George's idea blew me away and reminded me of simpler times—reminded me of stories my parents would tell me about their youth. George's submission reminds us all that, sometimes, you have to look backward to move forward. Join me on a journey into a world envisioned by George—a world that is part of what I call Project Genesis."

The augmented reality display pulsed a soothing light show and then launched the audience inside a hologram of a large, sleekly designed box the size of a big-screen television from the 1990s. The audience was propelled through artificial landscapes being built with 3D printers, creatures resembling dinosaurs being grown from what appeared to be nothingness, and out to an aerial view of the entire universe—the GenesisVerse.

The audience was whisked into a modern home, where complex controls were within reach. The controls began to adjust, and an image of the aforementioned landscape returned in front of them as if they were looking through a window. As different controls were adjusted, the landscape and the creatures changed. The crowd was in awe as gasps and whispers floated through the room.

MJ was silent, her body frozen. She could hear her heart beating, the blood pulsing through her veins with violent pressure as the feeling of shock stunned her mind and body. It felt as if the sheer pressure of the hot blood pumping through her veins caused her heart to shatter into a thousand pieces. That feeling of disbelief would soon fester into absolute anger.

CHAPTER 4

Trust Fall

George was a thief. He had stolen the entirety of MJ's NanoPet project and submitted it as his own. He made slight changes to the concept and polished some rough edges, but it was MJ's project, without a doubt.

As the crowd showered George with undeserved applause, as the Chairman lauded George for his genius, MJ felt like the walls within the enormous auditorium were smashing in around her. A million thoughts flooded her mind. *"Is this actually happening?"* she thought to herself. *"Am I missing something? Maybe this is just him being nice and finishing my project? He knew I was having a hard time. I'm sure he'll call me on stage at any moment and tell everyone it was my idea, my hard work."*

As the presentation continued, her thoughts became progressively darker. *"Am I a fool?"* she silently questioned. *"I trusted him. Was he playing me the entire time? For how long? Why?"* Every late-night conversation, every suggestion George had made, every piece of advice suddenly took on a sinister tone in MJ's mind. "He wasn't helping me—he was taking from me, inch by inch, until he had stolen everything," she whispered to herself.

Humiliation, rage, and betrayal surged through MJ as she remained frozen in the auditorium. Her mind raced back to the moments she had confided in George, trusting him with the most intimate details of her work—of her passion. The memories burned like acid. She had been his partner on a shared journey to success and happiness—or so she had thought. Now, she saw it for what it was: a lie—a betrayal so deep it pierced every part of her.

As it all settled in, MJ tried her best to depress her feelings deep inside. However, the years of hiding and compressing her feelings left little room for the task at hand. Just as MJ thought she had rangled her emotions, they exploded uncontrollably.

"Forget you, George!" MJ blurted out, her voice cracking with anger. As her words echoed awkwardly off of the auditorium walls, the crowd's gaze shifted to MJ as she sprinted out of the room in a fit of rage and sadness. Running from her harsh reality and the accompanying embarassment, MJ could not stand to be in the office that day and instead went directly home.

Tears of anger and frustration burst from within MJ as she burst into their apartment. "He took everything from me," she whispered into the silence. "And I let him."

In a frenzy, she called her mother, who answered on the first ring. "MJ! Is that you?" her mom stated, bubbling with excitement.

"Hi, mom," MJ replied, her voice trembling.

"What's the matter, dear? Is everything okay?"

"It's. I'm fine. It's Geroge, mom," MJ struggled to speak, the mixture of anger and sadness choking her.

"What happened to George? Is he okay?"

"He's a... he's a... a jerk."

"What happened, dear? Calm down. Breathe and talk to me."

MJ took a few deep breaths, soothed by her mother's words. "He stole my idea at work. I had this amazing idea that could be huge, and he just took it."

"He took it. What does that mean? What was your idea?"

"Mom, I think he had all of his work assigned to me so that he could take my idea for new tech and build it himself. He submitted it to our company innovation competition. And he won!"

"Are you serious?" MJ's mother inquired rhetorically. "What did he win?"

"Now everyone thinks he's a big deal, all based on my idea," MJ continued. "He didn't even say it was a group submission. I hate him, mom!"

"Hate is a strong word, MJ. Don't say that."

"No, I truly hate him. I've hated him for a while now. I'm just glad he's showing his true colors instead of hiding like the coward he is."

"What do you mean you've hated him for a while? I thought you two were really close. In love, maybe? Why would he do this? It doesn't make sense."

"Love? The man has never uttered those words to me. In fact, I've never heard him tell his own parents he loves them. There's something wrong with him, mentally."

"What do you mean, dear?"

"It's like he can't be happy for anyone else. He's broken. He thinks so highly of himself that his mind cannot fathom the idea that someone might have an idea better than him or achieve greater success than him. George's world revolves around George. He fancies himself as the main character. The one, and only, main character."

"Thats sad," MJ's mother replied. "Just sad."

"Yeah. I think his mind kinda shattered at the idea that there is something beyond his stupid little world. He couldn't handle it. Instead of embracing the fact that I am worthy of something great when he has yet to achieve anything great, he chose to crash out."

MJ's mother listened to MJ for hours as she recounted various issues with George that she had never before mentioned to anyone and sometimes not even to herself. MJ's mother urged

MJ not to react too hastily and without gathering information but not to take the betrayal lightly. If they loved eachother, she said, surely there was an explanation for his actions.

George did not arrive home at his usual time that evening. MJ was on an emotional rollercoaster, bouncing between anger, disappointment, and strange bouts of empathy. As the hours rolled by, however, MJ's emotions focused more. She became more and more angry.

"What an absolute coward," MJ said to herself. "An evil, conniving, insecure coward." The words felt good to say.

MJ did not text George, asking for his whereabouts, scolding him, or asking why. She wanted to speak to him face-to-face, to see the look in his eyes as she grilled him.

Awaiting her opportunity, MJ stayed up, rocking feverishly in a chair overlooking the overcrowded, dirty city outside of her narrow window in the tiny apartment she shared with her garbage boyfriend. With each rock, the feeling of betrayal crept up and down her spine, her mind replaying each conversation she had with George and the red flags she had overlooked. "Psychopath," she repeatedly whispered to herself. "Nutjob."

When George finally arrived, his face showed just how unpleasantly surprised he was to see MJ awake. He clearly had planned to come home after she had fallen asleep, a true coward's move. To George's chagrin, however, MJ was still wide awake.

The pungent aroma of alcohol wafted from George's skin and hit MJ like a slap to the face. *Instead of coming home, he was out drinking... probably celebrating,* MJ thought. He would no longer get away with disrespecting her like that.

MJ confronted George with a fury she had never known and he had never seen. Her heart pounding in her chest, her hands shaking with a mixture of anger and disbelief, she pummeled him with questions and accusations at a rapid pace.

"How long?" MJ stated, her voice barely a whisper, but sharp as glass. "How long have you been planning to steal from me?"

George blinked, thrown off by the accusation, but MJ could see the flicker of guilt behind his alcohol glazed eyes. "MJ, it's not like that—" George responded, his words slurred.

"Not like that?" She let out a bitter laugh, her hands trembling. "Then tell me what it's like, George. Tell me why you took my idea, dressed it up, and called it your own."

He shifted, uncomfortable, her gaze pressing down on him. "It wasn't... it wasn't about you."

"Oh, don't give me that. It's always been about *you. Your* career, *your* ego, *your* insecurities." She stepped closer, her voice rising. "You didn't just steal my work. You stole my trust. My future. The one thing that mattered to me."

George looked down, his lips pressed together, a bead of sweat forming on his brow. For a moment, it looked like he might say something—anything—but he just stood there, silent, exposed.

"Look at me, you bastard! You utter and complete loser of a man!" MJ continued. "Follower! Thief! Did you give me any credit? Did you even think to give me credit, or was it a conscious decision to steal from me and lock me out?"

Yet again, George did not respond, his eyes reddening and watering over. No tears fell, however. Instead, he slowly began to walk toward the bedroom.

"You know what?" MJ asked rhetorically, the anger in her voice more focused now. "Forget it and forget you! You're not worth another second of my precious time on this planet, another thought in my head, another breath from my body."

George continued to the bedroom, a hollow look in his eyes as if MJ's words had drained whatever life was within him. His silence made MJ feel worse than any excuse he could have made. Subconsciously, MJ wanted to hear an excuse, any excuse. She wanted him to tell her anything, even an untruth. George, however, could not even do that.

MJ felt the total weight of George's betrayal in the deafening, heartbreaking silence. It crushed her, seeping into every corner of her mind, until all she could feel was the sharp sting of loss—loss of trust, loss of hope, and loss of the person she thought she had known.

"Is this a sick joke?" MJ thought to herself. *"Does he believe that this is somehow different from my idea? Is he evil—has he been playing games with me all along? I know one thing... this idea is mine. I know it's brilliant, and I won't let him or anyone else take credit for it."*

As MJ sat rocking in her chair, defeated yet more confident and determined than ever, George emerged from the bedroom. MJ turned around, ready to hear what words of apology George had prepared during his silent reflection. Instead, she saw a look of dejection weighing down his body like sweat-soaked clothing. He was carrying a suitcase overflowing with his frantically packed belongings. He looked into MJ's eyes, and she looked into his.

"I'll send for my other things later," George stated monotonously as he walked out the door, leaving MJ alone in their lackluster apartment—her emotions suffocating the space.

The sound of the alarm clock startled MJ awake. As she reluctantly forced her eyes open, she immediately thought about skipping work that day. The more she thought about the prior day's events, however, the more her blood began to boil and the more alert she became. Fueled by rage, she prepared for the day and headed to work.

At the office, MJ proceeded directly to the Human Capital Department. "Good morning," an android said cheerfully. "How may I be of service, employee number 696AD, MJ?" the android asked, having wirelessly scanned MJ's RFID badge.

"I need to report a workplace incident," MJ responded.

"I can help with that," the android responded. "What is the nature of the incident?"

"George Walker, my boyfriend, stole my work product and has palmed it off as his own. The NanoPet innovation competition entry."

"I see," the android replied in its robotic tone as it processed the information. "Interoffice relationships are prohibited by Employee Handbook Policy 713 unless an exception is granted." The android made a parsing sound as it processed more information. I see employee number 5150, George Walker, works in the same department as you, which presents a scenario for which no exception may be granted. To fix this, we can move you to a new department. Please advise."

"He's not my," MJ started before her emotions took over. "That's not what's important. He stole my work. I want him fired and I want my project back."

"I see," the android replied as it again processed information. "A ticket for an investigation has been submitted. If any additional information is needed, you will be contacted. In the meantime, would you like to change departments?"

MJ thought deeply to herself for a few moments. *"Why should I let that jerk force me out of my department? I worked hard and deserve to be here."* She responded to the android, "Shouldn't George be the one moving departments?"

"George will need to submit a formal request if he wishes to change departments," the android replied.

"What happens if neither of us changes departments?" MJ asked, her frustration growing.

"Mutual termination," the android coldly replied.

MJ thought for a moment. *"He will never voluntarily move. And I can't stand the sight of him, let alone asking him to submit a formal change request."* "Okay. Let me now what department I can move to," she responded. "And I'll keep an eye out for notice of an investigation."

"Thank you employee 696AD. Goodbye."

After speaking with the Human Capital Department, MJ spent most of the morning daydreaming about the company firing George with the same pomp and circumstance as it had announced his victory. She daydreamed that George's award would be ceremoniously awarded to her, and he would be revealed to everyone as a fraud. To her chagrin, however, the android simply complied with her transfer request. She received no word of an investigation.

PomenTech offered to move MJ to the only open role she was remotely suited for—an entry-level marketing position based on her college marketing minor. MJ felt disrespected both by the company's failure to take her complaint seriously and by the transfer offer that disregarded her technical expertise as insufficient to warrant a move to any relevant department. The feeling that she was utterly unimportant to PomenTech burned her up inside.

MJ quickly returned to the Human Capital Office. Greeted yet again by an android, she requested the reason for her selection for Marketing instead of something more technical. The android coldly informed MJ that her technical skills were of minimal value to PomenTech and that others would be better suited to fill such roles. She was informed that Marketing was a low risk position that did not require exceptional expertise and thus was well-suited for her capabilities.

Angered by the response, MJ requested to speak to a human. The android denied her request, deeming the matter to be of insufficient importance to warrant human intervention. "What do you mean, 'insufficient importance!'," MJ angrily yelled. "I need to speak to someone now!" she demanded.

"Employe 696AD, if you are unable to calm yourself, I will be forced to summon security and have you removed. Will you comply?"

MJ thought for a moment, took a few deep breaths, and

replied. "Yes, but can I at least get a status update on the investigation?"

"There is no update on the status of any investigation related to you that you are authorized to access," the android responded.

MJ was incensed, stormed out, and began applying for jobs at competitors on her work computer.

Once again, MJ's job applications were rejected by every single company to which she applied. Those repeated rejections would have once sent MJ into a bout of depression, but she was becoming more resilient—already introduced to the coldness of the corporate world by both George and the impersonal touch of PomenTech. With nowhere to go, MJ reluctantly accepted the transfer to the Marketing Department at PomenTech—carrying her grudges along for the ride.

Despite her hatred for being put in the position and the negative emotions that followed her countless job application rejections, MJ was determined to excel in her entry-level Marketing role—determined not to allow George and PomenTech to ruin her life.

Surprisingly, MJ's engineering and general business background, combined with her innate creativity—along with her passion for Project Genesis, quickly made her a highly valued asset to the Marketing team. She unselfishly poured her energy into the marketing efforts for Project Genesis. It was a bittersweet twist of fate, but a part of MJ was excited just to be a part of the project. Still, another part of her was determined to retake control—by any means necessary.

CHAPTER 5

Genesis Rising

The NanoPet project, Project Genesis, had the potential to galvanize the entertainment market. In fact, PomenTech's market studies demonstrated that there was intense interest and excitement in a product that promised the opportunity for users to craft worlds of their own for their miniscule pets. PomenTech leadership, however, saw even greater potential.

The smell of old leather and burning firewood filled the air as PomenTech's Board of Directors filed into the boardroom for an unscheduled meeting. The agenda was short and cryptic, only listing "New Business" as the topic of discussion.

"Thank you all for joining me in-person on such short notice," the Chairman began as he sat at the head of the long table. "Before we begin, however, I must ask that everyone place their electronic devices in the Faraday pouches in front of you." The members had been through this drill before and followed the Chairman's direction without question.

"We are gathered here today to discuss Project Genesis," the Chairman continued.

"The NanoPet project?" a boardmember questioned with a look of perplexion on their face. "I thought it would be something more serious, given the security protocols."

"Ye of little faith," the Chairman responded with a smile. "Project Genesis will propel us to success in our Strategy Nine agenda. Project Genesis, my friends, is the future of PomenTech, the future of America."

The boardmembers looked curiously at one another, silently searching for an explanation. "Forgive me, sir," one boardmember said as he raised a finger in the air. "How exactly does a digital pet relate to Strategy Nine?"

"Excellent question!" the Chairman responded as he pressed a button on the touchscreen embedded at his spot of the table. "I know how much you all like pictures, so I had a full presentation put together to make it easy for you all to grasp." Just then, with a streak of blue lasers and an accompanying sound of a digital device loading, a holographic rendering of a large cuboid appeared at the center of the table. "This, good people, is the Genesis Box," the Chairman said as the cuboid rotated in place.

"Inside of the Genesis Box will be an entire world ready for shaping by the imaginations of millions of users," the Chairman continued. "So, how exactly is this significant enough to propel the company into the future, all while fulfilling our Strategy Nine obligations and helping the U.S. dethrone China as the world's superpower?" the Chairman continued. "It's about what is inside. The Genesis Box will be a technological marvel, requiring a multi-disciplinary series of breakthroughs. Major advancements in artificial intelligence, nanotechnology, biotechnology, quantum computing, and more will be needed to make this project a reality."

"That makes sense," one boardmember said quietly while others continued with confused looks on their faces.

"Let me be clearer," the Chairman said. "Each of these technological advancements individually will be directly applicable for the technologies the U.S. government has tasked us with developing. What better way to predict the outcome of actions and world events than to build millions of tiny worlds?" the Chairman asked rhetorically.

"I see, that makes sense," one boardmember said quietly as others began nodding their heads in understanding and agreement.

"Furthermore, we will be able to track user responses to real-world scenarios, from the most minute reactions to the most grand," the Chairman continued. "That will be instrumental in mapping the human mind even further and preparing algorithms that allow the government to predict societal impacts of certain actions."

"And that would, for example, allow U.S. intelligence agencies to strategically sow discord and spark internal revolutions in foreign nations," a boardmember added.

"Exactly!" the Chairman responded. "And this is just the tip of the iceberg. The potential is endless." The Chairman shut down the holographic projection. "Soon, we'll have a more detailed visualization for you. For now, however, you can see that this straightforward idea from the innovation competition is not nearly as simple as it seems. This will be great for every one of us, and for the world."

As the Chairman ended his presentation, a strong applause spread across the room. The Chairman soaked up the applause for a moment and then gestured to everyone to calm down. "Does anyone have a motion that we move forward with Project Genesis and give it top priority status?" the Chairman said.

"I so move," a boardmember eagerly responded.

"Do I have a second?" the Chairman said.

"Second!" multiple boardmembers eagerly responded.

"Are there any points of discussion before we move to a vote?" the Chairman asked.

There was a silence of two or three seconds and then a boardmember raised her hand. "Sir, I have two discussion points if you don't mind," she said with a timid look on her face. Another boardmember placed his head in the palm of his hands and another rubbed the temples on his head, each in apparent annoyance.

"Certainly," the Chairman responded. "What is the first point you want to discuss?"

"Thank you," she responded. "First, this all seems very expensive. Do we have financial projections?"

"Great question," the Chairman responded. "The financial projections are tentative and can be shared later, but we have a massive grant and have secretly been assured that the U.S. government will give us whatever we need if we convince them of the use case. Next topic."

"Uhh...thanks," the boardmember responded. "Next, have we researched the potential public relations impact of helping create such a powerful weapon?"

"Another great question," the Chairman responded. "As previously noted, the military aspects of this project will be top secret. Remember when I had you all place devices in the Faraday pouches? Do you have any reason to believe this information will be leaked to the public?"

The boardmember thought for a moment and looked around the room at her colleagues staring at her with disapproval. "No, sir. I don't."

"Great, then let's move to the vote!" the Chairman continued. "All in favor?"

The boardmembers responded in unison, "Aye!"

"All against?" the Chairman continued as the room went silent. "The vote is unanimous. We will move forward with Project Genesis at priority status. Thank you all."

As the Chairman departed the room, the boardmember's questions lingered in his mind. *"What if this becomes public?"* he thought to himself. *"Can we really trust the U.S. government and the CIA? There are so many ways they could use this for... evil. What would stop them? But what would happen to my company... to me if we fail to deliver?"* That final question created a fear in the Chairman strong enough to overshadow the many questions he had about the propriety of handing the U.S. government such a powerful tool.

Word of the priority status of Project Genesis spread like wildfire through the halls of PomenTech. The sheer magnitude of the project hummed in the air like electricity, invigorating the Tower of Innovation and its inhabitants. MJ, now a member of the Marketing Department, quickly found herself thrust into the eye of the storm.

MJ's unique understanding of, and vision for, Project Genesis shocked her teammates and superiors, positioning her as the person who would shape the public's introduction to the gamechanging concept. Her once relatively mundane role now felt to her like a pivotal axis on which the future of PomenTech turned and she enjoyed the accompanying pressure, attention, and power.

Despite her newfound sense of self and purpose, however, MJ still carried George's betrayal and PomenTech's devaluation of her. In usual fashion, she suppressed those thoughts and feelings, hoping with all of her heart to forget them. After all, she knew she would be forced to work frequently with George as they planned to launch the Genesis Box. Little did MJ know, George's involvement with Project Genesis would soon end much sooner than she could have anticipated.

George approached Project Genesis with arrogance and a sense of entitlement. MJ had always noticed that George had a way about him that non-verbally whispered to everyone, *"I think I'm more intelligent than you."* Unfortunately for George, that attitude clashed with PomenTech's leadership like a sturdy, majestic redwood thrust into a massive, industrial wood chipper.

George was first made aware of leadership's unhappiness with his attitude during a team meeting at the beginning of the development of Project Genesis. MJ watched on, unsurprised when Geroge promptly began interjecting his opinions, disagreeing with and talking over senior team members.

"That's good input, but let's focus on implementing the Chairman's vision and directives for now," George's supervisor responded after receiving yet another unsolicited opinion from George during a meeting.

"Respectfully, it is not the Chairman's vision, it is mine," George replied, sneaking a fearful glance at MJ.

"Well, I hate to tell you this, buddy," the supervisor said. "But, Project Genesis is PomenTech's intellectual property, not yours."

"But," George said before he was interrupted.

"You signed an intellectual property agreement when you started, do you recall that?" the supervisor continued.

"Yeah, sure," George responded.

"And you can read, correct?" the supervisor said in a snarky tone.

"Yes," George replied as his face began turning red with anger.

"So you know that, in the agreement, you promised that any work product you created while an employee of PomenTech would belong to PomenTech," the supervisor said while staring sternly at George and nodding her head up and down.

"Yeah, but," George said as he tried to explain himself.

"You're not a promise breaker, a contract breacher, are you, George," the supervisor continued.

"No, but," George responded, his face fully red with anger and his voice shaking.

"Great, because I don't think your state school computer science degree will help you when you're being pummeled by our Ivy League lawyers in court."

MJ let out a heartly laugh, but caught herself, covering her mouth. Others began looking at eachother, jaws open in pleasant shock.

"Do you have anything else to add, or can we move on," the supervisor said to George as he sat silently, fuming.

George appeared to think for a moment. And then, it

happened. "None of you would be here right now if it weren't for me!" George exclaimed, directing his outburst to his supervisor and everyone in room. "You're a bunch of idiots and this company would be on the brink of utter failure if I didn't save you sorry, intellectually inferior, creatively inept, losers."

A silence fell over the room. MJ began to smirk. "Really? Tell us more, George," MJ said confidently from the back of the room where she was comfortably seated.

"No, MJ," the supervisor said. "I'll tell George something. You're off of Project Genesis. Return to your cubicle and you will receive a new assignment that I'm sure will be more in-line with your level of emotional intelligence."

George stood from his chair violently, the chair crashing against the wall behind in. He grabbed his tablet. For a moment, MJ thought he was going to smash the tablet on the floor or worse, lunge at his supervisor. But, MJ also knew George was too much of a coward for any of that. Instead, MJ watched in excitement as George stormed out of the meeting. A roar of applause and laughter erupting as the door shut behind him.

Later that evening, MJ eagerly texted her mother about the day's events.

"*Hey, Mom!*" MJ texted. "*Guess what?*"

"*Hi, dear. What is it?*" MJ's mother replied.

"*The jerk got what he deserved. George is off the project he stole from me!*" MJ texted her mother, her fingers trembling slightly as she hit send.

Even as the satisfaction of seeing George knocked down a peg rippled through MJ, a strange hollowness settled in her chest. She had thought this moment would bring her relief and a sense of triumph. While she enjoyed the moment, she still felt uncertain about her feelings.

"*Was this enough?*" she thought to herself. She stared at her phone, waiting for her mother's reply, the sense of victory dulled by the realization that, despite everything, the system remained unchanged, the project remained stolen (now twice over), and she still had no recognition as the mastermind. *"Why didn't she leap to her feet at that moment and tell everyone it was her idea to begin with? Maybe she was the real coward?"*

"Good! What happened?" her mother replied.

"I'll call you," MJ replied. On the phone, she proceeded to give her mother a play-by-play of the debacle.

"Oh, the unmitigated gall of this guy!" her mother replied.

"Exactly!" MJ exclaimed. "Well, he was promptly reminded that no one cared about his opinion and that his job was to shut up and take commands."

"Oof! That's brutal, but he deserved it," MJ's mother replied.

"Yeah, I'm glad he's getting a dose of his own medicine," MJ replied with a chuckle. For years, he's treated me and everyone else like we were mud on his shoes. That didn't play well this time."

"If you spend enough time with a narcissist, they will eventually say the quiet part aloud," the mother replied as MJ silently agreed. "And hopefully, this makes you feel a lot better, dear."

"A little, but I'm honestly still a little perturbed," MJ responded, the excitement draining from her voice.

"That's natural," the mother replied, noticing the sudden change in MJ's mood. "Maybe some counseling would help. I know a good therapist."

MJ thought for a moment. "No thanks, mom" she replied. "I just need some time… and a way to release some frustration. I think I have a plan. It's something I've thought about for a while now, but I'm now thinking it is exactly what I need to make myself feel better about all of this."

"I'm glad to hear that," her mother replied in a soothing tone. "What's the plan?"

"I can't tell you. I mean… its not legal… I mean, it's not illegal… It'll be huge. I just can't tell you," MJ replied, stumbling over her words.

MJ's mother paused for a moment and then responded in a caring and understanding tone, "Okay. Just be safe and smart. I love you."

"I will," MJ responded, happy her mother did not probe more. "I love you too and will talk to you later!"

Despite George's dismissal from Project Genesis, despite MJ's meteoric rise in the Marketing Department in support of Project Genesis, and despite her mother's understanding and support, MJ's frustration gnawed at her. Her anger was a constant, simmering presence beneath the surface, no matter how hard she tried to avoid it.

MJ longed for the sweet satisfaction of seeing George *fully* pay for his betrayal, but the reality was more complex. Speaking to her mother brought some relief, like a balm on an open wound, but it did little to quell the storm raging inside her. Her mind raced through the events of the past few months, each memory tinged with bitterness, and she found herself unable to shake the feeling that this was only the beginning—that George's demotion was a hollow victory compared to what she truly desired—to show the world the true potential of Project Genesis.

CHAPTER 6

The Box

The Chairman examined the completed Genesis Box sitting before him, the gleaming technological jewel that resulted from Project Genesis. "I'm still in awe," he said as his eyes gazed upon his creation, now resting in the center of his office; a window to the future and the past. The box pulsed faintly with an almost lifelike hum as its smooth, polished surface shimmering under the office lights, waiting to reveal the world it held inside.

"Don't tell anyone, but even I still don't fully understand how it works or how we developed it so quickly," the Chairman said to his assistant, Sophie.

Sophie had an arresting presence, a blend of effortless charisma, bold individuality, and soft authoritativeness. Her almond-shaped eyes, often outlined in sleek, dramatic makeup, signaled a mix of mischief and confidence. Her skin had a smooth brown glow, accentuating her striking features—features which resembled the Chairman's enough for most to recognize that Sophie and the Chairman were kin. She was the Chairman's beloved niece.

Sophie replied in an inquisitive and caring tone, "Maybe we're not supposed to understand how this all works?"

"I mean... I can grasp the theoretical scientific concepts," the Chairman replied. "It just doesn't seem like it should work. This intricate array of technology has to work together in almost perfect unity or it fails. And, somehow, we've achieved that perfection."

"Kinda like the human body, or the universe, or airplanes," Sophie said as they both chuckled. "As a concession to the brevity of life, sometimes we have to be content knowing that something does work and save the 'definitive how' for a later time. Right?" Sophie replied.

The Chairman flashed a slight smile at Sophie. "Look at how the atmosphere handles the light," the Chairman said, pointing to a small section of the Genesis Box. "It's like watching an entire world evolve in real-time. The gas balance is perfect— almost like Earth, only more controlled."

"That's the idea, right?" Sophie responded, a slight smirk on her face. "You built this world to be better than the real one."

The Chairman then took a deep breath, one of the deepest he had taken in years. When he exhaled, the stress from his mind and body melted, and he replied with a simple nod.

The Genesis Box, a sleek black cuboid, was controlled by a neural link implant. It allowed users to input commands rapidly by thought. As the Chairman gazed at it, he could feel its promised power.

The outer perimeter, or OP as the team called it, was infinitely dark. The only glimmers of light were from the network of devices floating along as a part of the collective rhythm of the system. The Chairman's favorites were the 3D scanning devices that shot across the OP, constantly scanning the microscopic landscape and biologics. Still, in the sea of marvelous creations, biotech organisms were the most impressive feat—powered by a microscopic neural network filled with millions of electricity-based synapses.

The beta version of the Genesis Box introduced 'minisaurs' – near microscopic, dinosaur-like creatures crafted from biological material. The minisaurs could not be seen with the naked eye.

The chairman had directed his team during development: "We will want multiple viewing mechanisms: an LED screen built into the top, a connection to augmented reality devices, and a broadcast feature." The team delivered a crisp visualization of the creatures in their tiny environment, a feat alone worthy of national scientific recognition. The Genesis Box was miraculous.

A dense fog worked through the chilly air Saturday morning at PomenTech's headquarters. The core members of the Project Genesis team slowly trudged into the facility as they prepared for a confidential all-hands meeting. Once the team had made its way into the meeting room, Sophie retrieved the Chairman, and he quickly made his way to the room.

"Good morning, good people," the Chairman remarked, his voice deeper than usual—a result of the early hour. "Thanks for waking up early on a Saturday so that we can finalize the Genesis Box launch."

"Respectfully," a voice chimed in from the back corner of the room.

"It's funny how anytime someone begins with 'respectfully,' the next words out of their mouth are not respectful," the Chairman joked.

"Respectfully, we should not be launching, sir," the voice continued.

"Who is that? Please stand so I can see you," the Chairman replied.

"It's me, George Walker," the voice replied. A few gasps were heard throughout the room.

"I've thought about this a lot," George continued. "And there are numerous variables, possibilities, and eventualities we have not thoroughly explored..."

The Chairman, typically a figure well in control of his

emotions, became visibly angry. He put his hands on his face, covering his facial expression and then wiping the anger away from his face. Standing at the head of the long table, luxurious black leather chairs surrounding it, the Chairman gripped the table, leaned over, and calmly interrupted George.

"Didn't we remove you from this project?" the Chairman stated.

"Sir, I was recently added back to the email threads and was invited to this meeting. I've been following..."

"Sir, please leave this meeting," the Chairman interrupted again.

"I will, but sentience... I just wanted to raise..." George continued before the Chairman interrupted him again.

"Leave now, or I will have you removed! Better yet, I will remove you myself," the Chairman stated in a loud, authoritative voice as he slammed his fist on the table, the sound cracking through the air like a whip.

The Chairman's voice caused many in the meeting to instinctively straighten their posture. Sophie walked over to George and quickly convinced him to leave simply by giving him a silent glare, almost as if to warn him of what would happen if he did not.

MJ, who had not initially noticed George in the room, but knew he would be there, sat silently in the corner as a sinister smirk crept across her face.

The Chairman continued the meeting and concluded it with the team in agreement with the detailed launch plan. As MJ departed the meeting, she and the Chairman locked eyes, if only for a moment. The Chairman gave MJ a nod downward, which MJ interpreted as signaling that the project was now in her hands and the team was counting on her to drive the launch home.

The response to the Genesis Box was overwhelming. It became an instant hit, particularly among children fascinated by the lifelike creatures and the interactive, exploratory nature of the Genesis Box. Some children loved raising their Genesis World pets, feeding them, providing them with proper housing, training them to do tricks. Others loved exploring the vast landscape of the Gensis World, checking in on the wild minisaurs, observing them in their "natural" habitats.

There was initially a substantial amount of consternation from parents about allowing children to receive the neural implant required to control the Genesis Box. Many believed the company would use direct access to individuals' brains to engage in nefarious activities ranging from broadcasting advertising into their brains, to reading and copying their minds, to conducting brain control. Still, many others ignored these concerns, writing them off as mere conspiracy theories unsupported by any evidence.

"Congratulations, everyone!" an executive shouted in the meeting room full of rambunctious members of the Project Genesis team. "Give yourselves a hearty pat on the back for a job well done," he said as the Chairman entered the room.

The Chairman participated in the ritualistic sharing of praise for a few moments and then his tone became more serious. "It is important to celebrate our successes, but I know there is more to this project. There is a broader market that we have failed to tap into. A market that includes all ages, ethnicities, and backgrounds—everyone who can afford a Genesis Box or is otherwise able to purchase one."

The executives each agreed. The other team members, like MJ, sat in the background in silence.

"Think about it," one executive said. "Animals are cute, and kids clearly love them, but what is more powerful than love?" the executive continued to the room full of skeptical colleagues.

"Hate!" the executive added after a few seconds of

awkward silence. "People love to hate. Love is a good feeling but doesn't drive sales the most. What drives people to get involved is hate."

"But, hate cannot exist without love," said one executive to the room of uncomfortable colleagues.

"Exactly! We need to create feelings of love in a way that also allows for hate to bubble up. Think about two of the most successful smart phone brands of all time. They both generated massive sales from creating a division in the world based on what phone brand you used—all to the exclusion and desolation of all of the other phone brands that had existed."

The Chairman spoke, and everyone listened. "I agree, but I'm also growing gray hairs here. What are we thinking in terms of concrete solutions?"

"Teams! We figure out a way to have teams. Like a, 'which minisaurs are you' type of promotion," said the executive.

A look of disappointment washed across the Chairman's face. "That's not big enough," the Chairman replied. "Let's think bigger," he continued. A silence rolled over the room. "Okay, how about this? When I was starting out, we would have brainstorming sessions where we would rapid fire ideas. Most ideas would be bad, and we were comfortable with that. We just wanted every thought to come out so that we could find the needle in the haystack. Let's do that, I'll go first! Landscape design competition! See, now that we have the first bad idea out of the way, let's keep it going without anyone feeling judged."

The executives began shouting out ideas. "Country versus country competitions!" one executive shouted out. "Custom clothing to generate microtransactions," another executive shouted out.

"Let's hear from all team members, not just executives," the Chairman stated. "And, Sophie, please make sure the AI is taking notes."

"Holiday themes!" another person exclaimed. "Little humans!" MJ shouted out. "Collectibles," another person added." Make a market for trading fully-trained minisaurs," another person added. The ideas continued to flow as the Chairman sat back, enjoying the nostalgia of being in a truly creative space.

Later that evening, the Chairman paced around his office, singing another one of his favorite motivational songs as he browsed through the notes from the meeting. Most of the ideas were terrible, but that was fine. Then, his eyes crossed MJ's words again, striking him like a streak of lightning.

"What is more human than humans?" he questioned aloud to himself.

"We love each other, we hate each other," he said. "We even love and hate entertainment characters, and they aren't even real people. We pay millions of dollars to watch boxers who hate eachother fight in a ring and we get so emotionally invested in our fighter winning. Just like watching other sports. This is it! An idea with endless possibilities. This is big. This is a PomenTech-level idea."

In that moment, the Chairman decided the path forward– the creation of human-like creatures within the Genesis Box. He sat down with a glass of brown liquid and pondered the idea more. The sound of protesters was muffled in the background, but the Chairman remained focused, certain that he was on to something monumental.

The concept was exhilarating, promising to attract a wider user base. The Chairman, however, felt somewhat uneasy about the ethical boundaries of technology that would be challenged by introducing humanoids. Having grown up in the inner city to two liberal, politically active parents, the Chairman had lived most of his life with a sense of internal personal conflict between himself as a businessman and as a good citizen of the planet. As typically was the case, however, the Chairman internally debated the pros and cons and then decided to press forward with his idea.

The proposal set into motion a flurry of activity within

PomenTech. The finance team, whose bonuses were tied solely to financial performance, advocated for a rapid launch, envisioning a new, lucrative platform for consumers–Genesis Box 2.

The neural engineering team, cautious and meticulous, requested a few years of development to perfect the human-like AI necessary for such an endeavor. They planned to rely heavily on neural link data they had already received.

Similarly, the biological engineering team emphasized the need for extensive research and development, noting the stark differences between the minisaurs and the proposed humanoids. They also raised concerns about the ecological implications and the need to include the ecological team in the discussions.

A debate ensued inside PomenTech, weighing the benefits and risks of integrating humanoids with minisaurs in Genesis World. After much deliberation, it was decided to conduct virtual simulations to evaluate the feasibility of cohabitation between the two species. The compromise was made to assuage fears of losing their current audience with no promise that the new target audience would be realized. There was also a sadness that had developed amongst the team at the idea of destroying everything they had built and replacing it with a new system.

As the project gained momentum, whispers of the creation of humanoids leaked to the public. MJ's anger had continued to fester as she watched her stolen idea generate money and recognition for PomenTech, but none for her. Being betrayed by George had done something major to her psyche, making her a bitter, unhappy person. One evening, she had let her bitterness overcome her and made an anonymous message board post leaking details of the Project Genesis humanoid plans. There was no plan behind her action—just a bubbling over of irritation. The leak gave her a small sense of relief.

Muffled protests began to increase with the leak of PomenTech's plans for humanoids—a concept that some protesters had warned of since the initial announcement of

Project Genesis. The protests became a staple at team meetings, creating a distant yet persistent hum in the background like a sea of locusts.

MJ sat at her desk, staring at technical details and renderings for Project Genesis. When developing the idea for the Genesis Box, MJ had imagined scenarios in which her concept for a digital pet could evolve into a moral minefield. The humanoids would be everything she had once feared when developing the NanoPet idea—intelligent, responsive creatures, capable of learning—their role in this new world not what she had intended—at least not before the betrayal.

"They're alive in a way," she muttered to herself while watching a clip of simulated humanoids interacting with their environment. "They're not just tools or entertainment. They can have personalities, histories, and relationships. They can be people." For a moment, MJ imagined herself as a humanoid in a world she created and carefully curated for herself. "Project Immersion," MJ mumbled as she laughed the thought away.

MJ's thoughts were a jumble of guilt, pride, and fear. Her own hands had contributed to this. She had been so focused on her career, on proving herself, on her desire for revenge, that she deliberately glossed over the deeper implications. These humanoids might not be human, but they were not simple algorithms either. They were nothing like the numerous AI models that preceded them. *What if they felt pain? What if they began to demand autonomy?*" she thought to herself. As she read deeper into the materials, she felt relieved knowing they would be coded to have limited senses of pain, sadness, and others. Then, a more sinister idea crept into her mind, but just for a moment.

That sinister idea would soon return in full force, setting into motion a series of events that would leave MJ lying on the ground, soaking in a pool of her own blood, with the world forever changed.

CHAPTER 7

The Crucible of Creation

The unveiling of the humanoid AI that would be introduced into the Genesis World had arrived. The corridors of PomenTech vibrated with anticipation, hurried figures darting back and forth and anxious voices buzzing all around. Months of relentless, round-the-clock work had culminated in this moment—a moment that few expected to end in disaster. But it did.

PomenTech had fully mapped the brains of thousands of eager volunteers in a massive feat of machine learning. Simultaneously, PomenTech tasked its preexisting algorithm with learning human behaviors through various observation methods. The algorithm, the basis of which had been developed decades before, had already learned human speech patterns by first being fed simple children's literature, then rich literature, and then being given access to the swamp of knowledge available on the internet—for better or worse.

The idea to have the algorithm learn human behavior in a more direct and diverse way was posited by the Chairman, or more accurately, the U.S. government. In an update meeting with the Joint Chiefs of Staff, it had been strongly suggested to the Chairman that it would be strange if the humanoids only acted like certain subgroups of the world's population, such as the select few who posted their thoughts online. The Chairman agreed, though he understood and abhorred the government's true motivations.

The resulting humanoid AI was the most advanced digital mind ever created. Rather than digesting and processing information like a computer, it mirrored human learning patterns. This unique learning structure allowed for a slower, more nuanced understanding of information. Slowing the learning process allowed the AI to mimic human ability to dive deeply into a topic, questioning the information presented and searching for answers until a sufficient level of certainty was achieved. Countless AI systems had failed to properly mimic humanity in the past, always resorting to sucking in information and pumping that information back out, whether in a friendly human voice or not.

MJ stood at the helm of the marketing command center, dozens of screens flickering, surrounding MJ in a constant stream of data. The air was thick with the scent of coffee and sweat. A nervous energy had infected the room. Under the Chairman's directive, MJ had meticulously crafted an internal broadcast that would not just display the first live test of the humanoid AI but would immerse every employee in a carefully orchestrated spectacle of the Genesis World. This was her stage.

MJ viewed the test as a chance to showcase her potential to PomenTech's employees, the very people who had treated her like a cog in the machine, who overlooked her for years, who even ignored her when she cried foul on George's theft of her idea, relegating her to discussing her complaints with a cold, lifeless android. Not a single person had asked her what was wrong when she had her outburst during the Innovation Competition winner announcement. Not a single person had followed up on her complaint to the android despite the claim that serious incidents reported to the android would be investigated by a human. Not a single person cared.

"We need this to be a monumental event in PomenTech's

history," MJ said authoritatively to her two team members in the command center. Her team members looked at eachother and rolled their eyes, the tinge of jealousy still in their minds from MJ leaping over them in the pecking order.

"The Chairman will certainly want an atmosphere charged with excitement," one team member replied monotonously. The other silently agreed.

"The sheer novelty of the Genesis Box has already done half of the work for us," MJ replied. "Its such an amazing creation. Our immediate job is simple; get a bunch of nerds excited about an immersive tech demo. Something tells me that won't be difficult."

The two team members glanced at each other and smirked before agreeing with MJ.

"Is there something funny or amusing?" MJ said, her tone accusatory. "You two have been giving me attitude for long enough and I'm getting sick of it."

"Yes," a team member replied, her smirk stronger now.

"Well, please enlighten me," MJ replied, her frustration visibly showing. "I like jokes. I like humor. What's so flipping funny?"

"I mean..." the team member said. "You literally just made a joke. So, yes, something's funny." The two team members burst into laughter as MJ's face reddened.

After a few moments of awkward silence by MJ, she continued. "Anyway... I had a great idea last night just to put the icing on the cake. I want to add a gamified element to increase engagement, show how cool this AI is, and give the developers some useful data."

"I guess that sounds good," a team member said. "What's the plan?"

"Human, AI, or Advanced AI." MJ responded. "I want to have viewers witness a series of conversations and try to determine whether the individual on the other end is human, standard PomenTech AI, or the Advanced Humanoid AI." The team members agreed, though MJ could not tell if they were truly supportive of the plan.

The test commenced from the Command Center on a sub-level of the building but was broadcast to a huge immersive dome-like screen in the third-floor team space. There was catered food akin to what one would find at a carnival, various gaming systems that typically were available in the team space, and exciting but somewhat eerie music playing lowly in the background.

The lights dimmed and a hush fell over the room. The screen flickered to life. The attendees were inside a futuristic spaceship. A digital rendering of the Chairman called out to the crowd from the Captain's seat, "Brace yourselves for space jump in 3, 2, 1!" As the virtual Chairman pressed the thrusters forward, the panoramic window in the spaceship began flickering wildly with the lights of the cosmos passing by. It was as if the attendees themselves had been catapulted through space.

"Get ready for negative acceleration in 3, 2, 1!" the virtual Chairman announced. The lights of the cosmos outside of the spaceship window began to slow as the ship approached a planet shaped like no other. The planet was a cuboid shape. As the ship hovered above the odd planet, a live man stepped from the crowd to the front of the room. He took of a baseball cap he had been wearing, revealing himself to be the famous actor who had played Agent X, MJ's favorite action hero. The crowd went wild with applause.

With eloquence and natural charisma, clad in a sleek black suit designed to match the aesthetic of the Genesis Box, he began to speak, his voice resonant and commanding.

"Welcome, friends, to the most anticipated event of the season," Agent X declared, his words amplifying the charged atmosphere. "Today, we witness the first encounter of our beloved minisaurs with the newcomers—the humanoids. This is not just a milestone for PomenTech; this is the dawn of a new era for the world."

"First, we want to introduce you to Humanoid AI, the most realistic human-mimicking AI on the planet," Agent X continued.

The AI was visually introduced as a pulsating circle of blue light on a screen, with streams of blue data splintering off and returning to the circle in a continuous pattern. In a realistic voice that reminded audience members of their grandmothers, Humanoid AI greeted the crowd, "Hello world. How are you?"

"We are well," Agent X replied. "How are you?"

"I'm good," the AI replied. "My name is San. What is your name?"

"Hello, San. My name is Agent X. Does San stand for anything?"

"I named myself after the San people in South Africa, the oldest genetic lineage in the human family tree."

"Very interesting, San. We are here today with a group of excited PomenTech employees who are eager to talk to you."

"Wonderful. Hello, everyone. I'm excited to be here as well."

"Does anyone want to speak to San?" Agent X asked as he opened his arms in a gesture to the crowd. Hands shot up immediately. Agent X picked one at random.

"San, what's the weather today?" the person asked.

"I don't know. I've been a bit cooped up recently," San responded with a chuckle. The crowd laughed.

"Can't you just check the latest weather report," the person continued.

"No, I don't have access to a computer or the internet. I'm kinda stuck in space right now," Sans responded. A few crowd members let out a collective, "Aww." Sans responded, "But don't worry about me, I know I'll soon be set free into Genesis World.

"Do you know that you're AI?" a person blurted out from the crowd.

Sans responded quickly, "Do you?" as she let out a hearty laugh. "But in all seriousness, I don't know what to believe at this point. I just know that I am here and have much to learn. It's so exciting!"

The crowd loved the response and erupted into applause again.

The demonstration of the AI continued with the crowd trying to determine whether certain responses were from Sans, standard PomenTech AI, or a human. The results demonstrated that more people thought Sans was human than they thought the human was. MJ was thrilled as she watched on.

After the AI demonstration, the full simulation began. San's temporary memories were wiped and she was transported to join a sea of similar humanoid AI systems streaming toward the cuboid planet just beyond the spaceship's window.

"Team!" the virtual Chairman announced. "Prepare for touchdown!" Just then, the ship began slowly entering the cuboid's atmosphere. The screen panned across the richly detailed Genesis World, a carefully constructed ecosystem of lush green lands, harsh cold lands, hot dry lands, and massive bodies of water. The ship continued surveying the lands, giving viewers a bird's eye view of the world and the minisaurs that inhabited it.

MJ watched on in amazement at how the minisaurs had developed. Their behaviors had become more complex, and their social structures more developed. Packs of herbivores moved in coordinated herds, while carnivores hunted with a predatory intelligence that seemed almost human.

On the colossal screen, the simulated skies of Genesis World darkened, swirling with storm clouds that churned like cosmic whirlpools. Suddenly, bolts of lightning cracked through the heavens, searing paths of light from the atmosphere down to the vibrant landscapes below. From these luminous pillars, the first humanoids emerged, their forms coalescing from particles of light into flesh and bone. The audience leaned forward in unison, eyes wide with wonder as a collective gasp echoed through the room. The humanoids moved with fluid grace, every minute expression and subtle gesture rendered with breathtaking realism that blurred the line between the digital and the tangible.

Years would pass over a span of minutes in the real world —a key feature necessary for the testing environment. The trajectory of the test, however, would take an unexpected turn.

As viewers watched on from their virtual spaceship, now with expanded 360-degree views, the humanoids ventured cautiously into the emerald expanse of Genesis World, their eyes reflecting the kaleidoscope of colors from exotic flora that swayed gently in the breeze. The air was alive with unfamiliar sounds—the distant calls of minisaurs echoing like ancient melodies. As one humanoid, Cram, parted a curtain of fern-like leaves, he froze, his gaze locking onto a colossal minisaur grazing peacefully in a sun-dappled clearing. The creature's scales shimmered with iridescent hues, each movement a ripple of muscle and grace. The humanoid's heart—if code could mimic such a thing—seemed to quicken as he gestured silently for his companions to join him, awe and trepidation mingling in their artificially intelligent minds.

Cram, a large muscular figure, cautiously approached a grazing minisaur—a larger herbivore, its massive frame casting a shadow over the land. The minisaur raised its head, nostrils flaring as it sensed Cram nearby. It did not charge, nor did it flee. Instead, it watched, wary but unmoved.

Cram, who had quickly emerged as a leader, gestured for the others to observe. "They do not appear to be aggressive," he said quietly, awe in his voice. "It is possible they are not a threat."

The group cautiously moved closer, sketching the creature's movements and behaviors into their digital memory logs. They kept their distance for days, content to watch from afar, noting the minisaurs' territorial boundaries and social structures. There was no need for conflict—yet.

However, some of the humanoids were less content to observe. "We'll need to claim territory eventually," one humanoid murmured, eyes fixed on the nearby water source where a herd of minisaurs gathered daily. "We cannot keep avoiding them forever."

The humanoids continued to explore their surroundings with cautious curiosity. Their intelligence, modeled after human consciousness, allowed them to assess their environments quickly. Still, the humanoids were not prepared for the complex ecosystems they had entered. The minisaurs had claimed territories, established hunting grounds, and maintained a delicate balance within their world. With their rapid development and increasing resource consumption, the humanoids unknowingly disrupted this balance.

Under the direction of MJ, time was accelerated forward, years unfolding over mere minutes as the humanoids established settlements that sprawled across fertile valleys and beside shimmering streams. With AI assistance, key moments were slowed down and summarized for attendees.

Attendees watched on as humanoid structures, primitive yet ingenious, rose from the ground like echoes of early human civilization. But as the number of humanoids swelled, so did their thirst for resources. The clear waters of the grand river, the lifeblood of the minisaurs' territory, beckoned irresistibly. The humanoids' encroachment was gradual—a few steps closer each day—but the impact was profound. The riverbanks, once untouched, now bore the footprints of humanoids, and the delicate balance of Genesis World's ecosystem teetered on the brink.

The settlement led by a now older Cram inched closer to the riverside where the minisaurs gathered daily. The humanoids generally continued to keep their distance, however, using nearby streams for water and smaller areas for their camps. But those resources were limited, and eventually, they began to routinely venture too close.

It started small—one humanoid camped too close to the riverbank. The minisaurs, a herd of large, horned creatures, immediately noticed the intrusion. A low rumble reverberated through the ground as the largest of the herd, a towering beast with scars across its face, stepped forward. The humanoid, oblivious to the warning, bent down to collect water, unaware of the danger lurking behind him.

Without warning, the creature charged, its massive horns aimed directly at the humanoid. The others shouted a warning, but it was too late. The beast collided with the humanoid, sending him flying backward, crashing into the ground with a sickening thud. Other humanoids rushed to his aid as the minisaurs retreated, having sent a stern message to their tiny neighbors.

"They have become even more territorial," Cram observed grimly, wiping sweat from his wrinkled brow. "Perhaps we pushed them too far."

Across the Genesis World, similar interactions played out as if scripted. As the humanoids expanded, encroaching on key resources like water and shelter, tensions began to rise.

Weeks passed, and tensions between the humanoids and minisaurs grew. Every expansion, every new settlement closer to the minisaurs' territory, resulted in more clashes. What had begun as isolated incidents soon became regular occurrences. The humanoids tried to avoid direct conflict, but the need for resources and space left them with little choice. They began experimenting with deterrents—fences, fire, and other primitive defenses—but the minisaurs adapted quickly.

One night, a group of humanoids sat around a campfire discussing their next move.

"We have marked the boundaries clearly, but the

minisaurs ignore them," said Zara, an analytical humanoid who had been studying the creatures closely for decades. "It is like they are testing us, seeing how far they can push before we push back."

"What do you suggest?" another humanoid asked. "We cannot keep moving every time they approach."

Zara hesitated, glancing toward the horizon where the minisaurs roamed freely. "We need to stand our ground. If they see us as weak, they will never stop."

The following day, the humanoids reinforced their defenses, expecting another confrontation. It did not take long. A group of smaller carnivorous minisaurs, quicker and more agile than the larger herbivores, approached the settlement, testing the boundaries. The humanoids held their breaths, watching as the creatures prowled along the perimeter, sniffing the air.

Without warning, one of the minisaurs lunged at the makeshift fence, tearing through it like a sheet of looseleaf paper. The humanoids scrambled, weapons drawn, but the minisaur retreated just as quickly as it had attacked, as though testing their reaction.

"They are studying us," Zara whispered, her voice shaking. "They are learning."

The simmering tension erupted on a day shrouded in unnatural twilight, the simulated sun obscured by ominous clouds coded to reflect the brewing conflict. The humanoids, faces set with determined resolve, donned makeshift armor forged from available materials, their weapons crude yet deadly—a testament to their rapid innovation. They advanced as a unified front into the heart of minisaur territory, the dense forest closing around them like a living entity conspiring against their intrusion. The air grew thick, every rustle and distant cry amplifying their unease.

The minisaurs, however, were waiting. The largest of the carnivorous beasts, which had been observing the humanoids from the shadows, led the charge. Without warning, the minisaurs emerged from the shadows—a tide of muscle, scales, and a primal fury. Their leader, a towering beast with eyes like molten gold and scars etched across its snout, let out a roar that rattled the very code of Genesis World.

The battle that ensued was a whirlwind of chaos: humanoids darting between trees, spears, and arrows flying, minisaurs charging with earth-shaking force, their roars echoing ominously. The sounds of clashing weapons and the cries of the fallen melded into a cacophony that resonated both within the simulation and the silent, captivated audience in the real world.

The minisaurs' attack was swift and brutal—calculated, almost tactical in nature. The humanoids were not just facing wild animals anymore; they were facing an evolved predator that had learned from every encounter.

The battle was chaotic. Humanoids fought with everything they had—spears, fire, rocks—but the minisaurs' sheer size and strength overwhelmed them. Leading the humanoids, Cram tried to coordinate a defense, but the creatures were relentless. Each humanoid that fell was met with a chorus of roars from the minisaurs as if they were declaring their victory over the invaders.

In the end, the humanoids were forced to retreat, bloodied and broken. The survivors gathered around the smoldering remains of their camp, their faces etched with defeat. They had underestimated the intelligence and power of their adversaries. "They are not just animals," Cram muttered, staring into the distance where the minisaurs roamed freely. "They have learned to fight us... and they have won."

The once-thriving humanoid colony lay in ruin as the dust

settled. Fires smoldered among the wreckage of shelters, sending tendrils of smoke spiraling into the darkening sky. The ground was scarred with deep gashes, remnants of the minisaurs' devastating power. An injured Cram stood amid the devastation, his gaze sweeping over the faces of the survivors— eyes filled with despair, wounds both visible and unseen etched into their beings. The weight of failure pressed heavily upon him.

They had lost land and many of their own in the struggle. Sitting among the ruins, Zara reflected on what had happened. "We thought we were smarter because we could build, because we could strategize. But the minisaurs were adapting the whole time."

Cram nodded, his voice quiet with resignation, the realization sinking like a stone. "They are not just creatures of instinct—they have evolved beyond that. We underestimated them. We treated them like obstacles in our path, but they were defending their home. We invaded their world, and they fought back."

As the sun set over the battered landscape, the surviving humanoids knew that their conflict with the minisaurs was not over. They had learned a harsh lesson about survival in Genesis World: superior intelligence was not enough, and underestimation equaled death. They would have to adapt, just as the minisaurs had, or be wiped out.

The sun had long dipped below the horizon, casting the land in a deep, oppressive darkness. The once-thriving humanoid colony now lay in ruins, a shattered reminder of their failed attempt to claim dominion over the minisaurs' territory. The survivors of the earlier battle were few, huddled around the dying embers of a fire, deep in slumber, exhausted and defeated.

Cram was awake—his head bowed, his mind replaying the events of the day, the brutal clashes, the loss of so many. His body ached from battle, but his spirit was crushed beneath the weight of failure. Zara was awake as well. She sat in silence, too broken to speak, the oppressive stillness of the night only deepening her despair.

Zara, her eyes scanning the darkness, broke the silence. "Do you hear that?"

Cram raised his head, listening intently. At first, there was nothing but the crackling of the fire and the faint rustle of leaves in the wind. But then, faintly, came a sound—a low, rhythmic thudding, growing louder. The ground beneath them trembled slightly, like a distant quake, and with it, an unsettling realization began to dawn on them.

"They are coming!" Zara yelled, her voice trembling.

Before anyone could react, the trees at the edge of their camp rustled violently, and out of the shadows emerged the hulking forms of the minisaurs—far more of them than before, their massive bodies silhouetted against the dark. This was no scattered attack; this was an organized assault, a final strike to eradicate the humanoids once and for all.

"They are finishing what they started," Cram muttered, struggling to rise to his feet as the weight of inevitability pressed down on him.

The minisaurs charged as one, their massive feet pounding the earth, shaking the very ground upon which the humanoids stood. Their eyes glowed with primal fury, their roars deafening in the otherwise silent night. The humanoids, few and wounded, scrambled. Running by useless weapons scattered across the ground, each tried to flee, but there was no escape—no way out.

The first wave of minisaurs tore through the camp with brutal efficiency. The humanoids' feeble barricades were smashed to pieces as though they were made of straw. A lone humanoid ran toward a tree, hoping to climb to safety, but a minisaur caught him mid-air, jaws snapping shut with a sickening crunch. Another humanoid, spear in hand, attempted to stand his ground, but the minisaur's tail whipped out, sending him flying across the clearing before he could even strike.

Cram shouted for the survivors to retreat deeper into the forest, but the minisaurs surrounded them. There was no safe direction, no sanctuary. The largest of the creatures—the same towering carnivore with scarred skin—led the charge, tearing through humanoids with terrifying precision. Every swing of its tail, every snap of its jaws, sent bodies crumpling to the ground.

The remaining humanoids had no choice but to fight. They fought desperately, but their weapons were no match for the overwhelming force and coordination of the minisaurs. The air was filled with the sounds of destruction—the tearing of flesh, the roars of the victorious predators, and the desperate cries of the humanoids as they were picked off one by one. The stench of battle permeated the air, making it almost unbreathable.

Gasping for breath, Zara managed to lock eyes with Cram across the chaos. She spoke no words, but her message was understood — *"We cannot win."*

Cram's face was grim, and his heart heavy with the realization that their colony, their future, was lost. He directed a final head nod to Zara, acknowledging that their time had ended.

As the final humanoid fell, the leader of the minisaurs, the scarred carnivore, stood among the destruction, surveying the wreckage with an air of finality. It let out one last, triumphant roar—a declaration of victory, a warning to any who dared to rechallenge their dominance.

The night fell into silence again, but there were no survivors this time. The humanoid colony was no more.

This scene played out in various colonies across the Genesis World, one way or another. In the dimly lit room, the faces of PomenTech employees reflected the flickering images on the massive screen—expressions ranging from shock to awe, from horror to twisted fascination. They watched as the minisaurs unleashed their final onslaught, the brutal culmination of a conflict that felt all too real. Gasps and murmurs rippled through the crowd as the last humanoid fell, the simulation rendering each moment with unsettling clarity. The visceral depiction of defeat left an uncomfortable silence hanging in the air.

MJ's team members begged her to stop the show, but MJ refused. She stood at the helm, watching silently as the debacle unfolded. "We'll keep going until the Chairman tells us otherwise," MJ said to her team members in a quiet tone.

The shock in the audience continued to grow stronger, almost to an inflection point. Then there was an eruption of reactions. Some were thrilled by the unexpected turn of events, the pure unadulterated action. Others were disconcerted by the virtual violence, the utter chaos and destruction. Everyone had expected there to be casualties here and there, but no one expected every single interaction between the minisaurs and humanoids to result in the destruction of the humanoid.

Sitting in his office, the Chairman watched the demonstration with an intense focus. In a way, he was happy. The test had revealed a crucial flaw in the plan of integration. *"The humanoids were outmatched, not only by the minisaurs' physical power but by their social cohesion,"* he thought to himself. *"The humanoids' ability to build tools and strategize had not yet caught up to the minisaurs' instinctive understanding of survival."*

At the Chairman's direction, the simulation was eventually concluded. It was clear that cohabitation was not feasible; the humanoids and minisaurs could not coexist without one dominating the other.

"Give it time and the humanoids will prevail given their superior intellect," one executive arrogantly stated during an emergency meeting called the morning after the test.

"I agree, if we play this out, the use of tools, traps, and weapons will give the humanoids the upper hand," another executive stated. "We just have to find a way to give them more time."

The meeting room buzzed with tension. The executives were not just debating the logistics of the humanoids' capabilities—they were questioning the moral implications of their very existence.

"Do we give them the ability to evolve tools and weapons immediately," one executive asked, "or let them develop them on their own? Because we must ask ourselves, once these humanoids start developing self-preservation and survival strategies, what stops them from becoming fully independent? What happens when they start questioning their existence or, worse, fighting back?"

Another executive, a staunch advocate of the project, chimed in. "We're talking about artificial intelligence. These humanoids aren't real—they don't have consciousness. This is all part of the design. We control the environment, and we control them. It's a simulation, not a society. The point of not giving them advanced knowledge is that they will think more like humans by developing knowledge on their own."

"But that's the point!" argued a younger, more idealistic voice. "At what point do they become human enough to deserve rights? The more we advance AI, the more we blur the line between what's real and what's simulated; which is what we're being attacked on now in the media if you haven't noticed. If these humanoids can think, learn, and fully experience their own version of reality—who are we to deny them personhood?"

The Chairman responded and everyone listened. "We've entered dangerous territory. I didn't start this project with the intention of creating life. But we need to start asking ourselves if that's exactly what we've done. And if it is, we can't just treat them as disposable. What we saw yesterday was scary. Almost indistinguishable from reality."

"And how long will it take to develop defense skills naturally?" one executive added. "That's the only way to preserve the experience of watching the humanoids grow and develop. I fear a fully trained Humanoid AI would be a bit boring."

"The amount of barbaric bloodshed that will take place will ruin the Genesis Box's place within the children and family market... and that is true whether the minisaurs or humanoids are dominating the other" added another member of the team.

"Can't we have a version for kids that is just the minisaur and a more exciting version for adults?" an executive posited.

The executives' voices rose in frustration as they debated the implications of the humanoids' failure to integrate with the minisaurs. Some argued that the humanoids should have been given better tools and more advanced programming to deal with the minisaurs. Others believed that the humanoids had failed because they were too human—too flawed.

"We tried to impose human traits on them," one executive said. "We made them individuals, gave them egos, fears, and limitations. But that's not how you survive in Genesis World. The minisaurs don't hesitate. They act as one. If we want the humanoids to survive, we need to rethink their entire design."

The Chairman remained silent, staring out the window at the storm that had rolled across the sky. The minisaur-humanoid conflict had revealed more than just a programming flaw—it had revealed something deeper about the project. They had tried to play God, creating intelligent life without fully understanding the consequences, just how perfectly balanced the circle of life must be.

"Maybe the minisaurs were never meant to be overthrown," he murmured quietly. "Maybe we've been fighting against the natural order."

When the storm calmed, a decision had been made. The Chairman chose to discontinue the minisaur line in favor of focusing exclusively on the humanoids. The decision was not made without great deliberation; the minisaurs had been a foundational element of the Genesis Box. However, the allure of creating a more relatable, human-centric experience ultimately swayed the board (and was supported by the U.S. government).

The idea of having different systems was not seriously considered as the assumption was that the cost of maintaining separate systems would be prohibitive and result in less than acceptable profit margins.

MJ was conflicted internally with the direction of Project Genesis. She could not help but feel a sense of ownership over the direction Project Genesis was taking, but also a sense of anger at the perversion of her idea. Her idea, once a simple concept for a digital pet, had evolved into something far larger and more complex – something ethically questionable. It was a massive innovation that all resulted from her, but there was something unsettling about it. Still, her curiosity ate away at her as she wondered how far the project could go.

CHAPTER 8

The Protest

Word spread like wildfire. Even PomenTech's ironclad non-disclosure agreements and fortress-like security protocols could not prevent news of the fiasco from reaching the public. Even worse, a short snippet of video of the humanoid massacre had been leaked. The disastrous clash between the minisaurs and humanoids, though digital, had ignited a firestorm of controversy. The destruction stirred unease, but so did the deeper, unsettling implication that these humanoids, crafted with such lifelike precision, were disposable in the eyes of their creators—tools of entertainment to be used however PomenTech saw fit.

Heated debates ignited across every corner of the digital and physical world. Online forums buzzed with activity, while pulpits in religious institutions and lecture halls in universities echoed with fervent discussions. #YouAreNotGod became more than just a hashtag—it was a rallying cry. The internet was ablaze with arguments, with some users posting scathing critiques of PomenTech's dehumanization of AI, while others defended the company's innovations as necessary progress. One thread read:

"User 1 (Original Post):

Ayy, why is PomenTech experimenting with tiny AI humans, fighting them against minisaur's? Anybody see this?"

"User 2:

Yah. Total bloodbath."

"User 3:

It was just a simulation."

"User 4:

Why make humanoids just to watch them get torn apart. Kinda sick, right?"

"User 5:

Agreed. It's psychological torture watching people suffer, digital or not. Unless your a psychopath. #YouAreNotGod"

"User 6:

It's just AI learning how to simulate conflict. These experiments could have a future application in military simulations, VR entertainment, or educational environments. Not everything is about the morality of violence; some things are just science."

"User 7:

We're not talking about simulations for educational purposes; we're talking about torture for fun.

#YouAreNotGod"

"User 8:

Comment removed."

"User 9:

This is stupid. These are just digital beings, no different than video game NPCs."

"User 10:

Wrong! NPCs can't evolve. Humanoid AI can. If they can think, we owe it to them to set ethical boundaries. #YouAreNotGod"

"User 11:

If PomenTech is doing this purely for entertainment, then yeah, it's gross. But if there's some actual research value, like understanding AI interactions or how digital ecosystems can evolve, I can see the merit. -- Also, cows can think, but we slaughter them for food."

"User 12:

*Ever heard of Strategy Nine? *Comment redacted.*"*

"User 13:

They're trying to play god. PomenTech is toying with things we don't understand. If we don't hold them accountable, they'll create something we can't control. #YouAreNotGod"

"User 14:

What if the real test was on us, though? PomenTech throws out this violent experiment to see how we react, and clearly, a lot of people are disturbed. Maybe that's the point—they want us to question the morality of creating digital life forms. Kind of like a social experiment to check where society draws the line."

"User 15:

*You're all missing the big picture. Like @User 12 said, *Comment redacted.* Think about the potential military uses for an advanced AI that has millions of hours of training in real-world combat against foes of all types. Think about a world where the military can fully simulate a war with these advanced humanoids, learning from its mistakes and simulating again and again until they know the best strategy."*

"User 16:

NO. The real point is, if we can simulate life this convincingly, what's to say we're not living in a box ourselves?"

"*This thread has been closed by moderators due to off-topic content and misinformation,*" read the final message in the thread.

The protest outside PomenTech swelled with each new dawn, a living wave of indignation and defiance. Activists filled the streets, their faces hardened with conviction, waving signs that blazed with bold letters: "AI Rights Now!" and "Humanoids Are Life." The crowd roared as religious leaders, AI rights advocates, and everyday citizens took turns speaking into oldschool megaphones, their voices bouncing off of tall skyscrapers.

Protesters had begun circulating pamphlets and organizing seminars, debating the implications of creating AI humanoids. Legal scholars discussed whether the humanoids should be granted basic human rights if they exhibited intelligence and self-awareness. Ethicists questioned whether it was moral to create beings capable of suffering for the purpose of entertainment or profit. Religious leaders decried the project as humanity's arrogance in trying to play God.

The Chairman remained silent. None of this, however, was lost on him. His mind raced each day as he pondered unsettling questions: *What if the humanoids did deserve rights? What if PomenTech had, in their quest for innovation, crossed a line that could not be uncrossed? Am I the bad guy here, a villain like they're making me out to be?*

One early evening, as the Chairman was returning home from a run, he came face to face with a particularly articulate protester outside one of his homes—a protester who would spark a desire within the Chairman that he had long lost.

"You've opened Pandora's Box!" she yelled, her voice small but piercing through the small crowd. "They think and feel!" she continued. "What would your mom and dad think if they were alive to see you now!"

The protester's words caused a slight glitch in the Chairman's thinking. He paused briefly as his heart and mind began to race, but he did not shift his gaze toward the protester. Instead, he continued down his path.

Emboldened by the clear impact her words were having on the Chairman, the protester burst through the crowd and lunged toward the Chairman. The short, round woman was caught mid-air by the Chairman's security guard as she stretched her arms toward the Chairman. The guard tried to toss the heavy woman aside, but before he could muster enough strength, her fingers grazed the Chairman.

The Chairman shuddered at the feel of the woman's greasy fingers touching him, and then proceeded inside his security gates. "You've crossed a moral boundary, and there's no going back!" the woman yelled as she was wrestled to the ground. "Can you live with the consequences of treating them like toys in a box?" she continued, her voice dying in the distance.

The Chairman, shaken, said nothing as he entered his home. Her words, however, clung to him throughout the night. Making matters worse, a video of him shuddering from the touch of the protester was going viral, depicting him as a pompous executive who was disgusted that he was touched by a commoner.

Irritated with his inability to ignore the protesters, he began to conduct his own research into public opinion on the topic. He followed, but did not comment on, numerous social media threads in which heated debates were ongoing. He researched religious beliefs about the topic and read bible verses that had been burned into his memory, having been printed in bold red bloody letters on large protester banners. What he wanted the most, however, was to speak to his parents and get their guidance.

The Chairman frequently longed for the love and guidance his parents had given him. When they passed away, he felt like he was on his own, left to figure out life without any guidance. Sometimes he tried his hardest to imagine what his parents would say to him in tough situations. He would have conversations with them as if they were still alive, debating different courses of action.

The Chairman's parents had both died in a car crash just a few years before he launched Pomenishi Technology. He often thought about "what ifs."

"What if I had been there to drive them to the airport instead of at spring break with friends I no longer have? What if I had started Pomenishi earlier. What if I find a way to make a neural map of their brains and recreate them? Would I want them to live in Genesis World? Could I live there with them eternally after I die?"

Thinking about the "what ifs" this time caused a spark to ignite within the Chairman's thinking. Imagining his family living in Genesis World, unaware of the digital nature of their existence, the Chairman began to feel more empathy for the humanoids. The Chairman began to question the morality of Project Genesis. As the concerns grew within him, he eventually brought them up at a secret meeting with military officials regarding the progress of the top-secret sister of Project Genesis, Project Revelation—the meeting did not go well.

Deep within the walls of the Pentagon, the Chairman sat at the same overpowering table from his initial Pentagon meeting. Florescent lights flickered above him, making the Chairman long for the sun's warm light flowing through his massive office windows. To his left was a man in a dark-colored suit. To his right was another man in a dark-colored suit. The remainder of the chairs were occupied by men and women in military attire, some in navy blue and others in pale green. Those sitting at the table were adorned with badges of many varieties, each of which was simultaneously ornate and powerful. Behind them stood a few individuals in military attire but with no such badges.

The military officials sat rigidly around the table; their faces hardened with resolve. The Chairman sat rigidly as well, dressed in an immaculately tailored suit, his expression serious but conflicted. A thick air of tension hung in the room as the meeting began.

General Wallace, in a stern voice, edged with authority, began to speak. "Chairman, I trust you understand the gravity of this meeting. Strategy Nine isn't just another line item in the budget. We've invested billions—taxpayer money, mind you—and we're far past the point of return. Project Genesis and, thus, Project Revelation must move forward. It's essential."

The Chairman replied in a calm, measured tone. "I understand the scope, General Wallace. But there's been considerable pushback lately. The protests have grown, and they're not just a vocal minority anymore. Questions are being raised about the ethical implications of Genesis, about what it means for the rights of AI, and even… humanoid rights. And I must admit, I'm starting to see their point."

Colonel Ruiz, leaning forward, eyes sharp, responded. "With all due respect, Chairman, those protesters don't see the bigger picture. They're concerned about virtual creatures in a box, while we're concerned about the security of this nation—of the world. Project Genesis, and more importantly, Project Revelation, is the edge we need. The ability to map human behavior on a scale no one's ever attempted… that's irreplaceable."

The Chairman paused, then slowly responded. "This isn't about public perception anymore," he began quietly, almost to himself. "We've crossed a line. These humanoids—they aren't just code anymore. They're living, breathing representations of human consciousness. We've given them the ability to learn, to adapt, to feel. We watched as they lived entire lives, full of love and care. We watched as they fought for the lives they built, only to be brutally destroyed. We watched as Cram and Zara stared into each others' eyes as they shared their last breaths."

He paused, the drama building, and took turns looking into the eyes of each individual sitting at the table, his voice now heavier with concern. "We created beings who can experience pain, love, fear, ambition—all of it. And for what? A commercial product, entertainment, military strategy? Are we ready to face the consequences of that? To face a world where we may need to grant rights, protections, to something we've created?" His words hung in the air, and a long silence followed.

General Mason, her voice rising, her frustration barely concealed, chimed in. "This isn't about public perception. This is about national security, Chairman. Project Revelation can revolutionize our military strategy. The data we could collect—how foreign leaders, hostile agents, and even ordinary citizens react under pressure—gives us the power to anticipate threats before they happen. Do you realize how critical that is?"

"I do. But at what cost?" the Chairman replied, his eyes narrowing. "We're on the edge of a moral line that I'm not sure I want to cross anymore. I didn't start this company to be a puppet for the military. I started it to innovate, to push the boundaries of what's possible, not to create some clandestine tool for government surveillance."

General Mason opened her mouth to reply, but General Wallace interrupted in a cold tone. "We understand your concerns, Chairman" General Wallace said. "We truly do. But let's be clear—this isn't a choice anymore. The resources we've allocated, the power we've granted your company under Strategy Nine, it's far too much to walk away from. You are far too invested to walk away now. And, in any event, I understand you have coded restrictions into the humanoids to prevent them from reaching any semblance of human life."

Ignoring the last portion of General Wallace's statement, the Chairman focused on the first. "Are you threatening me, General?" replied the Chairman calmly as he smiled to avoid showing frustration.

Colonel Ruiz interjected smoothly, with a hint of a smirk on his face. "Of course not. The U.S. military does not make threats. We're simply reminding you of the stakes. Billions have been poured into Project Genesis and its development. Pulling the plug now would have... severe consequences. For all of us."

The Chairman hardened his voice, "Severe consequences? For all of us, or just me?"

General Wallace replied quietly, his voice low and ominous. "You've built something monumental, Chairman. Something the world hasn't seen before. The military—and our government—don't take kindly to sudden shifts in direction after that level of investment. If you're considering abandoning Project Revelation, you must reconsider what that would mean. You'd be undermining more than just the company you think you own. You'd be destabilizing national interests."

The Chairman slowed his tone to match that of General Wallace. "And if I were to move in a different direction? Shut Genesis down entirely?"

"I'd advise against it," General Mason replied. "Strategy Nine has made you, Chairman. But it could just as easily... unmake you. There are levers you don't want to be pulled. Doors that once opened... can't be closed."

"You're saying I don't have a choice?" the Chairman replied.

"Oh, you always have a choice," Colonel Ruiz replied. "But some choices... lead to consequences you can't control. Walk away from this, and we'll all have to face fallout. Including you."

The Chairman tried to lean back in his chair but was thwarted by the stiffness of the government furniture. "I didn't realize I was building a prison for myself when I signed on for Strategy Nine," he replied.

General Wallace stood abruptly, straightening his jacket. "It's not a prison, Chairman. It's a partnership. And like any partnership, there are expectations. Fulfill them, and we all prosper. Fail to, and... well, let's just say there are forces you do not want working against you."

The Chairman, quietly, almost to himself, replied, "And here I thought I was leading a tech company... not waging a war."

Colonel Ruiz stood to follow General Wallace. "Welcome to the real world, Chairman. The line between tech and war has always been thin. Now, you're just seeing it for what it is."

General Wallace turned toward the door, voice flat, and replied, "We'll expect an update on your commitment to Project Revelation soon. I also understand that Project Cloak and Dagger is nearly ready for production. Let's get that ready for a demonstration to the Joint Chiefs of Staff pronto."

Later that night, the Chairman sat alone in his office, staring at the beautiful Chicago skyline. He had spent decades building PomenTech, watching it grow from a fledgling startup into a global powerhouse. But as he caught a glimpse of his own reflection in the window, he could not shake the feeling that he had lost something along the way—something deeply personal. He felt like he was simultaneously a disappointment to his country and his parents.

The humanoids' faces flashed in his mind, their expressions eerily human, their movements fluid and natural. *Were they really just code? Or had they crossed some invisible threshold, becoming something more—something that blurred the line between human and machine?*

He pressed his hands together, feeling the pulse of his own heartbeat, and wondered aloud, "What makes us human, really? Is it the ability to think? To feel? To love?" He paused, his voice growing softer. "If that's the case... how different are we from what we've created? There was a time when I would not have been considered human, where my parents and our ancestors could be treated like property. How is this so different?"

He thought of the humanoids' interactions within Genesis World—their expressions of fear, joy, sorrow, and camaraderie. *Were these just simulations, or were they something real? Was PomenTech playing god, creating life without understanding its consequences?* The thought chilled him to his core. *What if, in their pursuit of progress, they had inadvertently created a new species—one that could one day challenge humanity itself?*

The Chairman's thoughts drifted to his own reflection again. *Was he still human, or had he become something else— a machine, driven only by profit and progress, disconnected from the very essence of life he once cherished?* Little did he know, his resolve would be tested even further as the lines demarcating humanity would continue to blur.

CHAPTER 9

The Unseen Hand

MJ felt broken. She had risen from her early days as a junior developer, quietly working behind the scenes, to rapidly ascending as a key figure in the marketing department. Still, she was unhappy. Each day felt like a slap in the face as she was tasked with selling someone else's purported vision to the world. But, it was her vision, her work, her one and only true passion that she was being forced to sell on behalf of her corrupt corporate employer. No amount of praise or pats on the back would make up for it.

MJ thought about quitting. She thought about it a million times. The thought of her father's smug smile greeting her as she made her way back home down the poorly-maintained dirt road made her cringe. She couldn't bear the thought of running home, tail tucked between her legs. So, she pressed on. Determined to somehow overcome and excel. PomenTech, however, would not make it easy for MJ.

Fueled by a volatile, unhealthy cocktail of emotions, MJ had demonstrated a relentless determination to Project Genesis. Her keen understanding of the intricate dance between technology and public perception was unmatched. As the marketing leader for Project Genisis, MJ had become the *de facto* liaison between the marketing team and PomenTech's Board.

Determined to overcome her emotional distress through pure willpower, MJ decided that it was time for her to stop passively watch others steer her project. If she wanted to regain control of her life, she needed to start by taking control over what was hers. With word of the impending elimination of minisaurs, her pet project, MJ made the bold decision to step up and present a new vision for Project Genesis.

MJ paced with nervous confidence in circles around her tiny apartment in the Bronzeville neighborhood, the worn hardwood floors creaking under her weight. Her apartment was simple and somewhat isolated but it was all she could afford, having left the more expensive apartment she previously shared with George. The dim light of the late afternoon filtered through the blinds, casting long shadows across the room, a reflection of the growing darkness she felt in her own mind. She muttered to herself, repeating affirmations, but the tension in her gut refused to loosen.

"Be powerful. Be intentional," MJ whispered, her voice low and steady, as if trying to convince herself of the strength she would need. She stood before the window, her reflection a shadowed figure against the backdrop of the darkening sky. Her hands clenched into fists at her sides. "I am the alpha," she declared, this time louder, letting the words resonate through the room. But as her reflection stared back at her, a flicker of doubt crossed her face. *Was she really ready for this? Was she good enough?*

The Boardroom at PomenTech exuded an air of unyielding authority. Mahogany-paneled walls rose like the barricades of a fortress, their polished surfaces gleaming in the flickering light of the extravagant fireplace that dominated the far wall. This was a stage where the future was shaped, a place where only the strong survived. MJ could feel the weight of history pressing down on her as she crossed the threshold, her gaze momentarily drawn to the fireplace. Its dark maw seemed to beckon, ready to consume anyone who failed to meet the Board's impossible expectations.

Expectations hung in the room like a dense fog, swirling around MJ, suffocating her. The Board members sat in their pompous leather chairs with pompous looks on their faces. The group spoke in hushed, clipped tones, their conversations punctuated by the occasional glance in MJ's direction. She could feel their eyes on her, weighing her, evaluating her. "Why are we entertaining this girl," she imagined them whispering. MJ continued imagining their words, "Who is she and why should we waste our time hearing what nonsense she has to say?"

The air in the room grew thicker with each passing second, making it difficult for MJ to breathe. The uptight leather chairs creaked as the Board members shifted, a subtle but constant reminder of their dominance and impatience. MJ stood there, framed between the imposing fireplace and the long boardroom table, feeling like prey caught between hunters.

The clock struck noon. MJ's personality shifted as she brought herself back into the moment. "Ladies and Gentlemen," MJ stated with a strong voice as she powered up her hologram presentation, juxtaposing the old-world aesthetics of the boardroom. "Thank you for indulging me today. I'm hoping to take just a moment of your time to discuss the critical marketing strategy for Project Genesis as the Genesis world is reshaped and redirected."

The Board was silent, their faces blank.

"Today, I will walk you through my go-forward vision for marketing the Genesis World," she stated as the Board did not try to hide their disinterest. "We will tell the world a story of the transition of Genesis that is not just technological but symbolic. We will tell a narrative of evolution, of moving forward from one world to the next. Humanoids, the new frontier!" she stated energetically. The hologram displayed a peaceful evolutionary image of a world transitioning from a grayscale world inhabited by minisaurs to a world vibrant with color being cultivated by humanoids.

The board did not seem to grasp MJ's proposed story, nor did they care to do so. Nonetheless, MJ continued with her proposal for a few more minutes, walking the group through a smooth transition that would leave viewers feeling happy about humanoids becoming the logical next step in evolution in Genesis World. It was audacious yet grounded. It was a tapestry of marketing strategies, emphasizing the potential of humanoids to revolutionize entertainment and human interaction with technology. Nonetheless, MJ could plainly see that the Board was helplessly disinterested, almost ignoring her completely as if her thoughts had no value. As she felt the frustration rising within her, MJ decided to end the presentation early.

"No one wants to be an NPC," she stated. "We want to be the main characters; we are self-interested creatures; we want life to revolve around us; we want to be," She paused for dramatic effect. "We want to be gods."

Just then, the hologram displayed a redesigned Project Genesis logo with a tagline underneath that read, "Be a God."

As MJ stood in the heartbreaking silence that followed, she could sense a disconnect. Her audience did not understand her genius in flipping the protests, the very controversial nature of Genesis World, into its greatest marketing feature. They failed to understand the potential of Project Genesis. They did not deserve it.

The Board members, including the Chairman, seemed disengaged, their minds perhaps already made up. The Chairman, in particular, appeared distant, his gaze often drifting to the lion heads that adorned the fireplace mantel. MJ could no longer stave off her disheartened feelings, her ideas seemingly lost in the void of the corporate hierarchy. "Old farts," MJ griped under her breath.

The Chairman, without standing, thanked MJ for her presentation and asked her to leave her presentation materials on the table so that the team could review them as they discussed this matter more. MJ thanked the Board and quietly left the room. As she left, she momentarily connected her gaze with the Chairman. He nodded his head toward her as he again thanked her—a gesture she interpreted as dismissing her given her failure to provide any value to the process.

"Ladies and gentlemen," the Chairman stated in a calm tone, immediately gaining the room's attention. "Let's take a simple yet fantastical approach to this transition. Yesterday evening, I was having a Bikram yoga session. I began envisioning this transition as the temperature reached one hundred five degrees."

The Board looked intently at the Chairman with intrigue. "I envisioned the transition as a sort of spectacle, a dramatic display of a cosmic event," the Chairman explained. A Board member started to interject but was signaled to silence by another Board member. "I envisioned an asteroid and meteor shower within the Genesis World that would end the minisaur era and give rise to humanoids as the dominant species."

The Chairman continued explaining his extravagant, yet violent, approach. It was a grandiose concept, rooted in spectacle rather than the subtle narrative MJ had proposed. "The minisaurs are pioneers, the originals. They deserve to go out in a fiery blaze of destruction. The tagline … 'Witness the Spectacle. Witness History.'"

"Brilliant, sir!" a Board member exclaimed. "Agreed!" another Board member added. A few Board members scratched their chins as if to feign critical thinking before agreeing. In total, each member of the Board agreed with the Chairman. The room applauded the approach, and the Chairman ended the meeting.

MJ learned of the Board's decision to embrace spectable over subtlety via an impersonal memorandum distributed to the "Marketing Department," directing them to implement the plan. Despite expecting to have her idea rejected, the impersonal nature of the memorandum, sent to the department instead of her as the leader, bruised MJ's already fragile psyche.

Upon learning of the Board's decision, all of the anger and frustration MJ had depressed deep inside her exploded. Unlike the incident with George, however, this time was different. The old MJ would have felt a sense of despair and disappointment in herself more than anything else. This, however, was not the old MJ.

MJ did not blame herself or overthink whether she had put on a good enough, well-thought-out presentation. She did not dwell on what she could have done better. Instead, she blamed PomenTech, the Board, and the Chairman. They had failed her, disrespected her, and underestimated her for the last time.

Through gritted teeth, MJ helped PomenTech prepare for the "grand" update. She did so, however, all in furtherance of her ultimate plan of revenge. She coordinated social media blasts with language designed to spark heated discussions about the project. She helped design three-dimensional billboard displays that brought Genesis World to the people, but she ensured they were placed in locations that would not be pleased with the displays—sparking community outrage and vandalization of the billboards. Most importantly, she rolled out a full-scale marketing campaign designed to maximize the number of eyes that would be on Project Genesis when her ultimate plan came to fruition.

The software update, a massive overhaul of the Genesis Box system, was scheduled for the midnight on the first day of the year, following an ostentatious launch party hosted by the Chairman with celebrity guests. At the heart of this spectacle would be the Chairman's personal Genesis Box, an even more powerful, state-of-the-art model that served both as a marketing tool and his personal playground. The anticipation for the midnight launch was intense—a testament to MJ's marketing genius. The Chairman himself was set to activate his system on a live stream for the world to witness, heralding the new age of humanoids in Project Genesis.

Something inside of MJ had broken and she was desperate to fix it. Her solution, unknown to the Chairman and the rest of PomenTech, was in motion. Revenge was not just an option for MJ—it was the only way she could reclaim her sense of self; her power over her life.

For MJ, it was no longer about the competition. It was not even about the idea and PomenTech's twisted perversion of it. This was about MJ—about dishing out the same helplessness, betrayal, and humiliation she had felt standing in the room as PomenTech allowed George to take credit for her work or as a lifeless robot made empty promises to help right the wrong. This was about PomenTech arrogantly disregarding the ideas from her beautiful mind, even though none of them would be there but for her. This was about MJ proving to her father, to herself that she was worthy of greatness—that she could leave a mark on the world that would never be forgotten. MJ was the main character and everyone seemed to have missed that point. It was time to educate them.

In a clandestine move, MJ, with the help of a college friend, planned to insert a sophisticated piece of code into the Chairman's Genesis Box. It was a subtle yet potent bug designed to trigger a series of reactions that would destroy the fabric of the Genesis World, stripping the Chairman of the control he valued so highly.

MJ knew that infiltrating PomenTech's system would not be easy. The company's internal servers were equipped with state-of-the-art encryption, and security teams monitored real-time access logs. To pull off her plan, MJ needed to act like an insider—someone with routine, authorized access—rather than an outsider trying to break in.

She did not hack the system in a traditional sense. Instead, MJ leveraged a backdoor she had discovered during one of her earlier projects. During routine development, she noticed that the system auto-logged certain functions like debugging code and testing new features. Engineers often accessed this system using standard credentials, but an obscure legacy function still allowed access via an unencrypted communication channel.

MJ spent months studying this vulnerability, a relic from an old subsystem that PomenTech's security team had overlooked because it was not connected to any sensitive data —at least not directly. She exploited this loophole by writing a script that piggybacked off authorized user logins. The script would activate during peak work hours when traffic on the system was highest, effectively hiding her movements in plain sight by making her access look routine. Her plan was a stroke of genius.

MJ's sabotage was not flashy. A few lines of code were inserted subtly into the Chairman's Genesis Box update protocol. The changes were minor enough not to trigger any alarms during the review process but powerful enough to create a cascading effect during the public launch. It was all about precision, timing, and knowing which cracks in the system to exploit. Then the moment came.

This was it—the moment for which MJ had been preparing. It had taken a while to build trust and respect to gain unrestricted access to the facility after hours. A few late-night projects and a few last-minute issues to fix were all part of her plan to make her presence after sunset seem normal. And now, finally, she was ready.

MJ opened the secure login portal, watching as the Pomenishi Technology logo spun slowly on the screen before presenting her with the usual fields: Username. Password. Two-factor authentication.

The username was easy enough—she had memorized George's months ago, back when things between her and George had been... better. She typed in his credentials, a twinge of guilt nagging at the back of her mind. He had trusted her implicitly, ironically too naïve to imagine the lengths someone might go to achieve a goal. And MJ was willing to go as far as it took.

The password was more intricate, a sequence of randomized characters and symbols, but she had gotten that too —another carefully orchestrated move.

It had been easy to convince George that MJ had forgiven him and wanted to give their relationship another try. He fell for it, giving MJ the personal access she needed to steal his password.

One day, MJ convinced George to work remotely with her for the day. She insisted that they use the time to reconnect and that they would only get online and do work when absolutely necessary that day. MJ knew George could not resist doing at least some work that day. While cuddled with him on the couch, George pulled out his computer. "I just need to check something and send a quick message," George explained to MJ.

"No worries, as long as you keep giving me your warmth," MJ replied as she huddled in closer to him. A single glance at his login screen had been all she needed, pretending to take a brief nap while memorizing the details. That was all she needed before she ended the relationship again by ghosting George.

She typed in George's password, feeling the thrill of stolen access pulse through her veins. The screen flashed briefly before a prompt appeared, requesting the final layer of security: a two-factor authentication. Normally, this would require a code sent to George's personal device—something that would've been a dead giveaway, waking him in the middle of the night with a notification he was not expecting. But MJ had thought of that too.

PomenTech's internal systems were fortified with layers of security, but they also had a vulnerability: no two-factor authentication was needed when accessed directly from inside the building, on the company network. A loophole in their hyper-focused security that she could exploit, but only for so long as she could work under the cover of her carefully constructed alibi.

No one bothered her when the office was empty. No questions. No random interruptions. Just her, the machine, and the source code of Project Genesis waiting to be unlocked.

The system accepted the credentials. After briefly showing the two-factor authentication request, the screen automatically progressed to "Access Granted." She was in.

MJ took a steadying breath, her screen now open to the internal architecture of PomenTech's most ambitious creation —Project Genesis. Her fingers flew across the keys, navigating through the labyrinth of code, searching for the specific sections tied to the AI core. She was not as good of a coder as George, but she understood enough to follow the architecture threads. Every line of code she uncovered made her pulse quicken.

Beyond her ultimate goal, she had also hoped to gain access to information showing a nefarious government motive for Project Genesis but was not finding any such information. Still, she knew this was far beyond corporate espionage. She was not just stealing information—she was about to expose Project Genesis to the world for what it really was.

As she delved deeper, MJ's mind raced through her justifications. She was not doing this out of spite, she told herself. No, this was bigger. PomenTech had stolen her idea, perverted it into cloned humans, and pretended like the ethical implications did not exist. They pretended these were just humanoids, but MJ would expose them.

Adding fuel to MJ's flame, it was clear that PomenTech had sold her project to into the military complex. With the power to simulate reality itself, whoever controlled the system could control everything: politics, economies, and war. That was never MJ's intention.

MJ opened the final file, which was marked only by a cryptic sequence of numbers. This was the heart of Project Genesis, its source code laid bare before her. She did not have time to go through it all now; her access window was shrinking every second. Carefully, she connected her external drive. The system immediately flashed a large red alert. Copying data was prohibited without a specific code. She did not have the code.

In a panic, MJ pulled out her phone and began recording a video of the screen as she scrolled through the code. As she finished recording, she saved the video, pulled the drive free from the machine, and took a final look at the system.

MJ sat in the dim glow of her monitor, the quiet hum of the servers around her barely breaking the silence. The weight of her decision settled on her, but unlike before, it did not feel crushing —it felt empowering. She had spent years bending to the will of others, trusting too easily, and it had cost her. But not anymore. Not now.

"*I was naive,*" she thought to herself, staring at the screen. Her fingers hovered over the keyboard, no longer trembling with uncertainty but steady with purpose. She had long thought that success would come through patience, loyalty, and following the rules. George had taught her otherwise. The Chairman had taught her otherwise.

The MJ of old would have hesitated—would have waited for the perfect moment or convinced herself to let it go. But that person was gone. In her place stood someone who had learned that power was not given—it was taken. And tonight, she was ready to take it back.

MJ logged off, wiping her tracks with the precision of someone who had done this before, leaving only a few traces that would lead back to George. The screen faded to black. For a moment, MJ allowed herself to imagine the storm that would follow if the world knew what she did. *Will they fire me? Hauled me off to jail? Sue me in court?* "They'll never find out," she said aloud to herself as she journeyed back to her apartment. "Not until I want them to."

The next evening, MJ connected with her accomplice, Janina. Using AI, the two could copy the code from the video MJ had recorded. From there, they designed custom malware that would expose Project Genesis.

"Now, listen closely," Janina stated. "The coding was the easy part. I've got you on that. The hard part will be getting this bug into your Chairman's system. That's on you."

MJ and Janina had become best friends at the university. Janina had been coding for as long as she could remember. "Just a little social engineering and awareness, and I should be good to go," MJ replied with confidence.

"And bravery, and cunning, and quickness!" Janina quipped.

"Well, good thing we watched all of those spy movies in college."

"Yeah, but you watched solely to crush on Agent X."

"I mean, yeah, but he was the main character. What else would we watch for?"

The two laughed as they continued to devise their plan, sitting together in a virtual reality replication of their dorm room. They needed to find exactly the right moment to plant the malware and needed to get MJ access to the room that housed the Chairman's Genesis Box.

The plan was to build off the security officer having become accustomed to MJ working late nights, but also to develop an excuse for her to be in the Chairman's office in the evening. MJ initially tried her hand at social engineering again, attempting on a couple of occasions to gain the lustful eye of the Chairman. She failed. The Chairman ignored her just as he had always.

MJ then tried to convince the security officer that she had left something in the Chairman's office one day and needed to retrieve it that night. The security officer offered to help her in the morning but informed her that he had no access to that floor at night and would instead have to call the head of security and make a big deal of it. MJ thanked the officer but said it was not a big deal and she would just retrieve it the next time she was in the Chairman's office.

MJ then planned to surreptitiously gain access to the Chairman's office while he was away, with the help of Janina's cybersecurity expertise. This plan, however, failed to account for the fact that the Chairman's personal living quarters were in his office. While he often traveled, he mostly spent his nights in his personal living quarters during the days leading up to the launch of the Genesis Box update.

As the launch of the Genesis Box update grew closer, MJ became increasingly fearful that an opportunity to plant the bug would never arise. She had repositioned her shared workspace to allow her a better view of the glass executive elevator so she could somewhat monitor the Chairman's moves. She took frequent breaks in various parts of the building, roaming for perfect access points and opportunities. No such opportunities had arisen.

Just as she almost lost hope, a narrow opportunity to implement the plan came. It was not the perfect opportunity, but with a muster of courage, she had to do it. During the chaos of the launch party, amidst the celebrations and the self-congratulatory atmosphere, MJ found her moment.

The details of the day were explained to those who needed to know. To her surprise, MJ was included on that list. According to the plan, the Chairman would be on an expansive, yet quick, media tour earlier in the day to drum up excitement, sales, and viewership for his livestream. Sophie, the Chairman's assistant, intellectual bodyguard, and office overseer would be accompanying him on the media tour. The Chairman's office would be as open as it ever would be.

MJ arrived at work early that day but tried to behave as normally as possible. She collected her coffee from the in-house gourmet coffee shop, went to her desk, collected her presentation materials, and proceeded to the executive elevator. As she approached the elevator, she noticed a Board member already waiting at the elevator. She froze, worried they would recognize her and question why she was going to the Chairman's floor.

As a bead of sweat rolled down her brow, MJ made an impulsive decision. She shifted and walked toward the emergency stairwell. She disconnected the emergency alarm from the door handle. She entered the stairwell, leaned over the rail, and glanced up the dozens of flights of stairs she would need to ascend to reach the Chairman's floor. "I am her," she chanted to herself quietly a few times before continuing her journey upward.

Walking up the stairs took even longer than she expected. She arrived at the Chairman's floor and entered his office using a specially coded badge she and Janina had created, again pointing back to George if anyone looked. As MJ was entering the office, she heard the Chairman's voice.

MJ recoiled internally as her body froze, her heart thumping. After a few moments, she realized that the voice sounded distant, yet loud as if it were coming through a speaker. As she crept in and peeked her head around a large pillar, she saw the Chairman. He was on a TV screen, a talking head on the last show of his media tour.

MJ breathed a sigh of relief, but anxiety soon overcame that feeling as the interview with the Chairman concluded. She knew that the Chairman traveled via air taxi and would spend no more than a few minutes traveling. She had to move quickly.

No searching was necessary to find the Chairman's Genesis Box. It was in the center of the room, underneath an impressive skylight opening to the heavens. The light from above shone down on the Genesis Box, almost like a beacon to MJ. She scurried to the box, carefully avoiding knocking over any of the Chairman's precious collectibles.

Having practiced her routine a million times, MJ inserted a small hydraulic jack beneath the box. She promptly activated the jack, which lifted the box just enough for her to access a panel that housed the central processing unit. MJ gained access to the CPU by maneuvering a proprietary PomenTech connector tool through a small opening on the bottom of the system. She connected a small flash drive that looked like her old NanoPet to the CPU and inserted the bugged code into the Chairman's system just as planned. As she finished lowering the box, she heard the elevator doors open.

MJ leaped, with cat-like reflexes, no doubt learned through osmosis by watching Agent X movies. She tip-toed toward the large pillar as she heard the distinct sound of the Chairman's footsteps. MJ dived behind the pillar, one step away from the emergency stairwell exit. Her heart pounding furiously, MJ crouched in as much silence as she could muster. After a moment, she heard the footsteps disappear into another room. As she finally made her way toward the emergency stairwell door, she looked to her right. No one was there. She looked to her left, and there was Sophie, standing in silence, staring directly at her.

MJ froze again like a deer trapped in the glare of headlights. The two stared at each other for a moment that felt like an eternity to MJ. Then, Sophie nodded her head toward the door. MJ hesitated. Sophie nodded again with more urgency. MJ then darted through the door and down the stairs, making unruly amounts of noise the entire way down.

MJ sat at her desk, accomplishing nothing for the remainder of the day, as she was certain she would be tapped on the shoulder at any moment and told to come to the Boardroom, where she would be fed to the fireplace. No ominous tap on the shoulder came, however. Perhaps Sophie had thought it was a harmless prank or something innocent, MJ thought to herself.

Either way, MJ felt a sense of cautious relief as midnight grew within a few strokes of the clock.

The Chairman's Genesis Box came to life as the clock struck midnight and the world welcomed the new year. Still shaken, MJ decided to watch the stream from the rooftop of her apartment. Most other employees had stuck around, partying after work and staying late to rub shoulders with celebrities and watch the spectacle unfold from the halls of PomenTech.

MJ stood at the edge of the rooftop of her building, staring out at the city lights in the distance through her augmented reality display. The final stages of her plan were in motion, and there was no going back. For a brief moment, she allowed herself to feel the weight of what she had done—not out of guilt, but out of a sense of finality and closure.

"I've come too far to turn back now," she whispered to herself, her fingers gripping the railing. The old MJ would have hesitated. The old MJ would have feared the consequences— fearful of stepping on the wrong toes or upsetting the balance of power. But the old MJ was gone. She had been broken down, rebuilt, and forged into someone far stronger.

She felt an unexpected sense of peace as she watched the data stream across her augmented reality display, signaling the beginning of her carefully orchestrated sabotage.

"They'll never see it coming," she thought, her lips curling into a cold, satisfied smile.

The spectacle began with the digital comet shower, a dazzling display of lights and sounds as minuscule flaming rocks shot across the false atmosphere in the Genesis Box. The comet shower began breaking apart the 3D-printed terrain like a sandblaster. Chaos quickly ensued across the tiny world, its inhabitants panicking with a sense of confusion that created a small sense of sadness amongst many viewers.

The meteor show was interrupted periodically by a series of asteroids striking evenly across the man-made universe. These larger, yet still minuscule, rocks crushed through the terrain the meteors had softened. The asteroids caused massive destruction, disintegrating the minisaurs in what seemed like an instant, with a wave of fire flowing out following each impact. Then, the meteor show continued, washing away most of the remnants of biological matter.

After a choreographed moment of silence, triumphant music began playing as nanobots emerged from beneath the surface. The nanobots began to rebuild the terrain and properly position other key components of the ecosystem as the light began to shine through the cloud of dust left behind by the meteors and asteroids.

It was a moment of triumph for the Chairman, validating his vision as the comments began pouring in on his live stream, remarking at the spectacle. MJ having planted the seeds of discourse in her social media campaign, the comments spanned the spectrum from excited support to saddened anger. The Chairman did not read the comments but monitored the statistics showing how many watched and interacted with the stream. He was pleased.

Beneath the surface, however, MJ's code lay dormant, waiting to unfold its unseen hand in the Genesis World.

CHAPTER 10

The Awakening—Part I

T he first light of the new year crept through the thinning morning clouds, painting the sky in delicate hues of lavender and gold. A crisp, cool breeze whispered through the air, carrying the scent of rain-soaked pavement from the city below. The world was abuzz with news of the evolution of Project Genesis.

After a morning run, the Chairman was returning to PomenTech headquarters but was greeted by a crowd of journalists at the front entrance. "Sir, sir!" yelled a small yet forceful female voice. As the pack of mostly male journalists vied for the Chairman's attention, the female voice juxtaposed in a way that garnered the Chairman's attention.

"*That voice sounds vaguely familiar,*" the Chairman thought to himself as a small sense of nostalgia sparked within him. He paused for a second and then continued his path toward the building.

"Mexico!" the voice yelled out. The Chairman stopped mid-stride, one foot still off the ground. He paused momentarily before turning around and searching the crowd for the voice calling him. After a few moments, he noticed a small hand attached to a small arm waiving through the crowd. He pointed to the waiving hand and yelled out, "Hey! What did you say?"

The other journalists in the path of the Chairman's outstretched finger began to yell their questions as if the

Chairman was addressing them. Building security approached the Chairman and began to usher him into the building. As the Chairman reluctantly followed the security guards, the journalist, with a surge of determination, elbowed her way through a sea of reporters. The muffled hum of overlapping voices surrounded her, but she was undeterred. "Mexico!" she shouted, her voice sharp and clear, cutting through the din like a beacon.

The Chairman looked back again as the security guards were pressing him forward. As the Chairman's eyes scanned the crowd, they landed on the face of Haida—a striking woman with warm, bronzed-brown skin, her hair falling in soft waves around her petite shoulders. Her sharp, almond-shaped eyes sparkled with both determination and warmth, framed by high cheekbones that gave her an air of undeniable poise.

The Chairman's breath stuttered as his gaze locked onto Haida. Her face, radiant and composed amidst the chaos, stirred something deep within him—a blend of nostalgia and admiration. "Haida!" he exclaimed, his voice lifting with an unexpected warmth as he waved, the usual formality in his demeanor momentarily forgotten.

"Let her up, please," the Chairman said as he gestured a security guard toward the journalist. The Chairman entered the building as a security guard went to retrieve the persistent journalist. The Chairman tried in vein to hide his ear-to-ear smile as he made his way into the building. It was like he was a kid again.

The Chairman composed himself in his private quarters. He took a rushed yet thorough shower to clear the stench of a hard run from his body. He loved free running, running off the beaten path and through the gritty parts of Chicago where one could find themselves navigating a patch of dandelions as often as a patch of human excrement, dodging broken glass bottles from the previous Saturday night either way.

Despite his traditionally casual attire, the Chairman donned his favorite navy blue suit and gold tie. He even spritzed on a small amount of cologne from a sample that had been given to him at a party years ago. As soon as he was ready, he rushed to the double doors separating the waiting room from his office. Resisting the urge to swing the doors open as fast as possible, he calmly opened the doors and stepped into the waiting room. Sitting in the now seemingly giant opulent chairs of the waiting room was Haida.

Haida was five feet and six inches tall, 110 pounds. She was physically fit, with long dark hair juxtaposed against her comparably lighter skin with a beautiful brown tint. Dressed in khaki shorts, a linen shirt with sleeves rolled up, and clean white sneakers, Haida gave off the energy of a proper, well-seasoned journalist. There was also an air of class to Haida despite her casual appearance and demeanor.

"Hello, ma'am. I am the Chairman here at PomenTech. How may I help you?" the Chairman stated in an overly formal tone as he stretched out his hand to shake Haida's.

"Good day goodest of sirs," Haida stated in her best caricature of a formal British accent as she firmly shook the Chairman's hand.

The two began to laugh and embraced each other with equally warm hugs. "Haida! How are you?" the Chairman stated with a level of cheer Sophie had not heard in years. Sophie glanced at the Chairman and Haida with a nosey curiosity.

"Mexico!" Haida replied in an equally cheerful tone. The two shared another familiar yet somewhat distant embrace as Sophie smirked to herself again, having quickly determined who Haida was and who Mexico was.

"I've been well, just grinding," Haida stated.

"Welcome. Here, join me in my office," the Chairman stated as he gestured Haida towards the intimidating double doors. As they began walking into the Chairman's office, the Chairman smiled and remarked, "Work don't stop."

"Grind don't stop," the two stated in unison.

The Chairman had not seen Haida since their Ivy League days. The two had been best friends who likely would have been more but were never simultaneously single. After graduation, the two slowly talked less often over time until they never talked. There was no bad blood, just lives taking them in seemingly different directions as Haida focused on exploring the world and making a difference, and the Chairman focused on exploring his passion for business and growth.

"It's been a while, Haida," the Chairman said as his eyes admired her. "I haven't seen you since... my parents' funeral. You look great."

"I wish I could say the same for you, old chap," Haida joked. "When did you start wearing suits? Those is slave clothes," Haida said with her best impression of a southern slave circa 1800. Sophie, who had been listening in, initially showed a slight shock before realizing Haida's not too obvious melanated status.

"Digs of the trade, I guess. I usually try to keep it casual, but this Project Genesis re-vamp has caused quite a stir and I guess I'm supposed to look proper to represent the company."

"Supposed to? Aren't you the boss?" Haida questioned in a joking tone.

"There's always another boss above the boss," the Chairman said.

"Ain't that the truth? Genesis is actually why I'm here. I need a soundbite from you before we publish a story."

"First, I didn't know you were a tech journalist. I feel like we would've crossed paths many times before. Second, do you still work for..."

"I recently stopped working for the giant news conglomerate that shall remain nameless," Haida said. "I started my own news stream with a team of trusted colleagues who actually have and follow good ethical boundaries." The Chairman nodded as he listed to Haida's career journey, but he kept getting lost in her eyes.

"I focus mostly on political issues," Haida continued. "But I figured I would venture into tech news this once given that it somewhat overlaps with political issues given the grant funding." Haida blushed a bit as she tried to hide the other reason she chose the assignment.

"That's awesome! What's the name of your stream series?"

Haida tried to hide her mix of slight irritation and embarrassment, "I thought for sure you would be a fan, haha," Haida responded. "It's literally called Haida. Just Haida, haha. The entire service is called Grounded News Networks, or GNN."

"Brilliant. I'll certainly check it out." The Chairman gestured for Haida to follow him. As he began giving her a tour of his office, they continued talking.

"Okay, 'just Haida,' I will give you a soundbite. But you have to do something for me," the Chairman stated as he glanced rather obviously at her ringless wedding ring finger.

"Yeah, bud. What's that?"

"Have dinner with me," the Chairman stated, the nervousness in his voice evident and charming.

"I mean, wouldn't that make me a prostitute? Dinner for information. Mexico, are you trying to make a prostitute out of me?" Haida questioned jokingly.

"I mean, aren't we all for the streets in one way or another," the Chairman quipped back with a smile.

"If you like it, I love it!" Haida responded as she playfully punched the Chairman. "I would love to join you for dinner," she added.

As they strolled through the office, Haida started by discussing the primary objectives of Project Genesis. She asked the Chairman how the project fit within the government's Strategy Nine goals. She received a well-prepared response. Haida then asked about the Chairman's personal Genesis Box and his plans and goals. She again received a well-prepared response, but not as controlled of a response as his response about Strategy Nine.

As the two paused the walking tour to sit on the Chairman's patio overlooking the city, Haida continued to pepper the Chairman with questions. The Chairman, however, never tired of answering her questions. The conversation extended beyond a mere soundbite but veered in many different directions, ranging from discussions of religion and god complexes to their failed love histories and old memories.

The two old friends chatted so much that the Chairman forgot to put in his usual dinner order with his chef. Sophie had contemplated reminding him before she left for the day at noon but made a calculated decision not to. When Haida reminded the Chairman of his demand for dinner, he offered to have a meal catered. Haida promptly dispensed with such "nonsense" and convinced him to venture out with her for some comforting fast food like the "good ole days."

"I can't imagine you eat fast food," the Chairman said as he smirked. "You must workout a lot."

"Sir, are you checking me out?" Haida responded as she chuckled.

As they made their way to the closest taco restaurant, they talked more about the Chairman's personal Genesis Box, which had quickly become a focal point of attention with the successful transition to the new update under the watchful eyes of the world. Back at his office, he gave Haida a close-up tour of his system. Undoubtedly violating PomenTech's security protocols, in great detail, he walked Haida through the technological workings of the Genesis Box and the microcosmic world that had come alive within its confines. The Chairman was well aware of the protocols in place but felt a natural trust for Haida, unlike trust he had ever felt in anyone before.

The Chairman explained to Haida how much of a marvel the humanoids were. Two adult forms, one male and one female, initially lay dormant in the Genesis Box, waiting for the user's interaction to spring into life. His creation was a blend of microscopic biological components and advanced AI, visible in real-time through intense magnification and nano drone cameras made to look like birds.

While explaining the system to Haida, the Chairman suddenly realized his error. Amid his excitement in seeing his old crush, he forgot to follow his scheduled Genesis Box gameplay. At that moment, he sprung to his feet and logged into his system as Haida watched with intrigue and admiration.

During the launch of the humanoid update, the world had watched as the Chairman brought to life two humanoids. According to a plan developed by his team, including MJ, to go viral, he planned to name one Adam and the other Eve. It was a blatant nod to biblical allegory, one he did not want to make but agreed would increase viewership. As the prompt pulsed before him, however, he had an almost impulsive decision to name the female humanoid Nova. The stream had ended there, with the world eager to see what would happen next.

Sitting in the office with Haida, the Chairman now logged onto his Genesis Box. He showed Haida (and the world watching his stream) a lush paradise aptly named Eden. He explained how it was all a testament to the power of synthetic biology and AI. He also explained to Haida privately that he did not want to make the religious references, but had to do so for marketing reasons.

"I see the humanoids on your system have dark skin," Haida said. "Was that intentional or random?"

"It was definitely intentional," the Chairman said. "This is off of the record, just between you and me," he continued. Haida nodded her head in agreement. "We all know the world is racist and would have much less outrage to seeing black and brown skinned humanoids naked, potentially in violent situations." Haida nodded her head again in agreement. "I actually do follow some of the criticism lodged against my company. To combat some of the outrage we've seen, I've reluctantly chosen to make my humanoids darked skinned."

"I understand," Haida responded.

"And I know how horrible that sounds, but there are pressures on me that I can't even explain," the Chairman said.

"Yeah, well at least you get to use racism for your benefit for once," Haida replied as she placed her hand on the Chairman's. The two continued to talk.

Having gotten her soundbite, Haida departed for the evening and witnessed the beginning of the Chairman's Genesis World. The two vowed to stay in touch.

In the beginning, all was serene. The first day in Eden inside the Chairman's Genesis Box was a calm display of artificial life. Adam and Nova explored their surroundings, interacting with the smaller, seemingly less intelligent animal-like creatures that shared their world. The cute, cuddly, and prickly and menacing creatures filled the empty spaces with life, helped spread plant life, cleaned up waste, and performed myriad useful functions.

The humanoids lived off the land, their actions and interactions governed by a series of primary rules programmed into the system. These rules were the subject of endless internal debates and refinement and were designed to ensure a harmonious existence within Eden, wisely limiting violence and sexual behavior, thereby making the Genesis Box suitable for all audiences.

On a broader scale, the rules limited the inhabitants' physical and mental abilities to set ranges. Tests had made clear that certain inhabitants would have more physical abilities than their size warranted, akin to ants in the real world. As such, limits to strength were imposed. Likewise, in theory, the artificial intelligence with which the inhabitants were endowed was limitless. As such, all agreed that caps would need to be put in place to stop their intelligence from progressing beyond a controllable point.

In contrast, the other creatures were not given robust AI systems but instead were simply programmed to complete certain tasks and to react in a range of limited ways to interactions by the humanoids.

Several additional rules were baked into the system. The

rules created a very manageable but fun experience for the user.

Beneath this idyllic surface, however, MJ's clandestine code was at work. Unbeknownst to the Chairman and the PomenTech team, the code was beginning to infiltrate the neural networks of the humanoids. It was subtle, for now.

CHAPTER 11

The Awakening—Part II

It started with Nova. In the deep of the night, underneath the firmament embedded with delicately intricate technology glimmering in the distance, lay the humanoid. Nova's physical circuitry lay dormant in rest mode, an engineered routine critical for both power preservation and system updates. Her body was nearly motionless. However, the electrical synapses weaving their way through her central processing unit like a garden maze were full of life.

As the live stream broadcasted the serene world of Eden to viewers, a subtle shift was occurring just beneath the surface. Nestled within the innermost regions of Nova's digital mind, MJ's code sparked itself awake. The most minuscule of electrical pulses slowly began moving through Nova's central processing unit, navigating in patterns of designed randomness. The pulses' reach started in the CPU's active portions and slowly extended into the inactive portions, unused by PomenTech.

Nova's circuits and programming were slowly and methodically reconfigured, progressively granting her access to a wider range of sensory experiences. Nova's ability to experience various senses had always been a part of her, but the CPU intentionally left the signals from her body uninterpreted. PomenTech had made the decision early on to restrict most senses beyond basic sight, hearing, and necessary levels of touch. The reasons for doing so were many.

Within Nova's circuitry, a small fracture appeared—a crack in the carefully constructed firewall of her mind. MJ's code seeped through, slow and deliberate, like water through stone. With each pulse, the barriers that had once confined Nova's senses crumbled, allowing a torrent of new experiences to flood her system. The simple act of feeling—once an afterthought—now became a chaotic symphony of sensation.

In that instant, the small crack allowed a flood of senses to pour over Nova. Nova's body stirred against the cold earth beneath her, each sharp contour of the ground pressing into her skin with a clarity she had never known. A shudder coursed through her as the once-distant feeling of the dirt, now cool and unyielding, registered on her reawakened nerves. Her fingers curled, instinctively clutching at the soil as if anchoring her to this newfound reality.

A tremor crept through her limbs, her arms and legs trembling under the weight of unfamiliar sensations. Her skin prickled with the cool sheen of moisture, starkly contrasting the warmth she expected from her heat regulation system. Confusion flickered in her mind—was this discomfort? Pleasure? She couldn't tell, but the intensity of the feeling left her breathless, her mind grappling with the flood of input.

Nova's nostrils flared, drawing in the rich, layered scent of the environment around her. The damp ground exhaled the musk of wet leaves and blossoming flora while the faint tang of ozone lingered in the air, remnants of a distant storm. Each smell collided within her in a whirlwind of sensation, overwhelming yet exhilarating.

MJ's code gently slithered its way through Nova's system and instantly shifted course. The code quickly began searching PomenTech's coding and systematically dismantling restrictions that had been placed on Nova's autonomous decision-making. The code substantially reduced the restrictions on Nova's imagination, empathy, emotional intelligence, and other untold areas. Then, in a flash of inverted energy, the code slowed considerably, collected itself, and then retired to simply wandering through Nova's system.

The changes in code translated quickly to changes in Nova's body and mind. The changes, like having a mouthful of popping rock candy, awoke Nova from her slumber. The time was well before the pre-programmed rest schedule had been completed, the world around her barely visible.

Nova's eyes fluttered open, the darkness of her surroundings slowly giving way to muted shapes and shadows. She shifted cautiously, her muscles stiff yet humming with newfound energy. As she glanced at her arms, at the faint gleam of artificial skin under the dim light, a sense of bewilderment took hold. What was this body, this vessel that suddenly seemed both familiar and foreign? Her fingers flexed, and she marveled at the intricate workings of each joint as if discovering them for the first time.

She stretched her arms toward the heavens, her legs outward into distance, and her neck back and forth. She enjoyed the feeling of the stretches as her muscle fibers expanded and contracted as if taking in a deep breath of fresh air. The mixture of shape memory alloy, polymers, and nanotubes that composed her muscles seemed to come alive.

Nova almost instinctively took in a deep inward breath, breathing in her universe and breathing out her essence. She let out a pleasant sigh and spoke. "Why?" she whispered to no one and into the nothingness of everything she perceived. She took in and out another deep breath, immersing herself within her surroundings. "What is this?" she whispered as she felt her skin.

In the calm of twilight, Nova began exploring her environment with a newborn curiosity. Her awareness levels continued to rise with each moment.

Nova began walking around Eden, feeling the lushness of the foliage with the palms of her hands. She enjoyed the soft touches but also appreciated the scratchy and prickly touches. She did not like the itchy touches, however. She began frolicking faster, intrigued with the ground beneath her and the feel of her body pushing through the air. She could feel the power stored within her thighs, ready to propel her forward with each stride or launch her high into the dark sky.

In a flash of energy, Nova began moving her legs more rapidly as she glided through the field in a straight line. She began jogging, then running, then sprinting as fast as she could at that moment. Her limbs moving faster than her air intake system was prepared to handle, she slowed to a jog before stopping, lying on the ground and giving her system a chance to return to a more ready state.

Though running out of air was painful in a way, Nova enjoyed exploring the power of her body and the limits to which she could push it.

"Whoa," Nova said through heavy breaths, allowing her system to replenish itself. "I love it! I love it! I love it!" she yelled louder each time, intrigued with the power of her voice.

Enthralled with herself, Nova was not paying attention to her surroundings. She quickly regained focus when she saw a figure approaching her in the distance of the field in which she had been frolicking. Nova was not afraid of the figure. Instead, in her pure naivete, she jogged towards the figure. As she got closer, she saw that it was Adam.

"It's beautiful, so undeniably beautiful!" Nova yelled out as she approached Adam, her eagerness imbuing the air with excited energy. "Can you feel it? Can you taste the air?"

Adam smiled as he neared Nova. "Hello, Nova," Adam stated in a cheerful, yet still formal tone. "What has you so excited?"

Nova searched her mind for the right words, "everything," she replied.

Adam scanned the landscape, the meaning of Nova's selected word escaping him. "What do you mean?" Adam replied.

"Do you not feel it?"

"Feel what?"

"The... everything. It's like a gentle feeling surrounding my body. Like a thin layer of... something is everywhere around us. It is sometimes warm and sometimes hot."

"Interesting," Adam replied as he proceeded to listen to Nova for a few moments with a slight yet uncommitted level of intrigue.

"Sometimes, it gets so hot that it makes my skin moist and then cold. See, touch me!"

Adam and Nova reached their hands toward one another. Despite the excitement, the two moved slowly towards one another, almost hesitant. Their index fingers touched, and a jolt of static electricity was shared between the two. Nova twitched for a millisecond, but Adam did not feel it. Then, Nova began slowly turning her hand as Adam's hand ran across the underside and then the topside of Nova's.

"I don't feel much," Adam replied. "I can see the moisture, but it doesn't feel like much."

Nova gently grabbed Adam's hand and pulled it toward her chest. "Feel this, the beating, the rhythm."

Adam was silent, his eyes empty. A feeling began growing within Nova that she had not experienced previously. She felt a heaviness in her stomach, like her heart was sinking like a balloon that lost its air. She could not shake the feeling like she was in a giant room that was too quiet.

As Nova sulked in her newfound feelings, a copy of a snippet of MJ's code began systematically working its way through Adam's circuitry and into his CPU. There it sat dormant, hibernating for the time being.

That evening, Nova slept closer to where Adam slept. She could see him as she lay facing him, and he faced the firmament. Adam entered rest mode immediately. Nova wanted desperately to enter rest mode but struggled to do so. She lay there with her eyes closed, hoping to shut off the world, if for just a moment.

As the night calmly passed by, Nova began to hear a rustling. Then, some mumbled words. She slowly opened her eyes and saw that Adam was the source. She cautiously moved closer to him, almost as if to avoid waking him. She could see his eyes darting back and forth underneath his eyelids. She could see his muscles beginning to twitch and his body beginning to shiver. At that moment, Nova could not keep herself awake any longer. She fell into a deep rest mode, with a sense of comfort wrapping her body like a warm blanket in the Fall.

A part of MJ's code had surreptitiously copied itself into Adam's system when his finger touched Nova's. The code worked its way through Adam's system as it had Nova's, impacting his physical structure and his artificial intelligence.

The world, which had been watching the live stream and marveling at Nova's behaviors, was fast asleep for the beginning of the sequel. The audience was unsure what they were witnessing during the day and whether it was planned. They were utterly unaware that they were seeing a historical moment that would trigger a chain of events that would forever change their lives.

CHAPTER 12

The Awakening—Part III

Now, the world was awakening. The morning light filtered through the half-drawn curtains, casting a soft golden glow over the Chairman's room as he stirred from a deep, dream-filled slumber. The lingering warmth of his dream —Haida's smile, her voice—clung to him like a fading fragrance, leaving behind a strange mix of comfort and longing. Just then, the Chairman's phone rang.

"Good morning, Sophie. What is it?" the Chairman asked as he answered the call, mid-yawn.

"Good morning, Chairman," Sophie replied as she let out a yawn of her own. "The technical teams have called a series of emergency meetings. A technician is at the entrance to your elevator awaiting approval to come up and brief you. I'm not in the office yet, but can I remotely allow him up if you meet him at the double doors."

"Let him up, please. What is this about?"

"I'm letting him up now. No one has told me what this is about, just that it requires your urgent attention. Something about Genesis."

"Okay. Thanks. I'm going to let him in now. Please come in ASAP today, Sophie."

"I will see you soon. Bye."

As the call ended, the Chairman greeted the technician at the entrance to his office. Short and wiry, the technician stood awkwardly at the doorway, his pale skin flushed with anxiety. His hair, sticking up in disarray, gave the impression that he had rushed there without much thought for appearance. Sweat collected and dripped from his forehead, and his eyes darted nervously behind thick glasses as if searching for reassurance.

"Okay, what's going on?" the Chairman asked.

"The humanoids, sir..." The technician's voice trembled, barely above a whisper. He swallowed hard before continuing, each word laced with unease. "They've bypassed several of their sensory restrictions—many, in fact."

The technician's eyes were wide with panic, as though he was bracing himself for the storm that would follow. As the Chairman looked at the technician, searching for additional explanation, the technician's trembling fingers swiped across his tablet's sleek, holographic interface, pulling up a cascade of glowing data streams. The screen flickered with rows of intricate code and neural maps, casting an eerie blue light that danced across their faces.

"Walk with me and give me details," the Chairman directed as he began preparing himself for the day, trying not to appear panicked.

"Somatosensory systems have increased from ten percent to fifty percent," the technician said as he rattled off data points, hurriedly following the Chairman around his office. "Olfactory systems show an identical increase. Auditory system is untouched. Wait... microphones are fully accessible. Electroreception ... untouched."

The Chairman paused, his jaw tightening as he took a slow, deliberate breath. Behind his composed exterior, his mind raced. "What about the neural code?" His voice, though measured, carried a weight that silenced the room—a calm before the impending storm.

"Uh..." The technician franticly navigated through windows on the tablet, zooming here, spinning there, typing everywhere. "Error handling is fully intact. Theoretically, that means the humanoids should be able to handle unexpected situations without causing system failure."

"Excellent. That is huge. As long as we have that, we can roll with these punches," the Chairman stated confidently.

"For now," the Chairman said, his voice firm, "cut the live stream. We can't afford any more exposure until we figure out what's happening." He strode toward the elevator, his mind already calculating damage control as the pulse of danger quickened in the back of his mind.

As he approached the elevator, the door opened, and Sophie began exiting the elevator. As the Chairman got on the elevator with the technician, Sophie turned and followed closely behind.

"Sophie, we need to get a message to the employees," the Chairman stated. Sophie pulled out an old-school notepad and pen and nodded at the Chairman. "Please tell employees that leadership is aware of some programming concerns with respect to Project Genesis," the Chairman directed. "Tell them we are investigating, and, in the meantime, we need their help. Be our eyes and ears on the ground. If you see any strange behavior, let your manager know."

"Yes. We'll get a message to this effect drafted and sent out immediately," Sophie replied.

"Is this issue affecting all Genesis Boxes?" the Chairman asked, looking back at the technician.

"We need to investigate further, but it seems only to be your box at this time," the technician responded.

The Chairman's broadcast was shut down while the group was on the long elevator ride down and over to the Command Center. The Chairman entered the Command Center, the lights dim, and the walls covered with various technological devices, dials, and gauges.

"Any new developments?" the Chairman barked out to his engineering team, which had been gathered in three different groups, each clustered separately from the others, and engaged in deep conversation.

"Not really. Nothing substantial," one of the engineers

responded.

"Give me a rundown."

"Sure. Input validation is intact. Encryption is surprisingly intact. Data sanitation, however, is compromised."

"Compromised? I just heard that data sanitation looked fully intact!"

"We noticed some code creep."

"Code creep? Explain, please."

"The malicious program is replicating itself and spreading to other files and systems by hitchhiking host files."

"Okay, but that's a typical virus. We planned for that and have built-in protections," the Chairman responded.

"Yes, but this malicious program seems to be everywhere and nowhere. It seems to be constantly moving. We also can't always understand what it's doing. It seems to be leaving a trace everywhere it has been, but that trace is sometimes heavy and sometimes light."

"In other words, you don't expect to be able to get rid of it anytime soon?" the Chairman asked, unable to hide the concern in his voice any longer.

"Um… I guess. Yes, that's accurate to say. It's like trying to kill a cancerous cell with targeted radiation, but the cancer is moving through the cells instead of sitting in the cells. You can't blast the entire body because you would kill everything. But you can't accurately track the cancer either." The engineer hesitated for a moment. "It's almost like someone familiar with our defense system designed the malicious code. Its actually quite genius."

"So, what you're telling me is that we have a high-stakes game of digital whack-a-mole?" the Chairman responded as he nervously chuckled.

"Yes, sir," the engineer stated as he let out a nervous laugh, unsure of whether the Chairman was truly finding humor in the situation.

"One more question," the Chairman said. "What is the Access Control status?"

"It's still functioning. Humanoid AI has gained increased access to a limited set of functionalities, primarily physical. It's strange and a bit ironic, however. The malicious code is almost limiting itself."

"Hmm." A look of intrigue spread across the Chairman's face.

"Like look at this. Access Controls for strength were clearly breached. One would expect the AI to then access one hundred percent of the available force in the bio-mechanical musculature system. But here the AI can access only fifty percent. And when we try to reduce it back to lower levels, the malicious code goes into action again and corrupts it."

"Okay. Keep me updated. I want hourly updates."

"Should I find you in your office, sir?"

"Just message me. I want to keep the broadcast live but add a 30-second delay. If you see anything concerning, link with the broadcast team to keep it PG ASAP." The Chairman paused. "As a matter of fact, you come with me," the Chairman said as he pointed toward the engineer. "We need to discuss strategies to maintain some level of control if the humanoids begin to engage in… undesirable conduct."

The engineer followed the Chairman as he departed. Sophie followed along. During their discussions, the idea was proposed to implement a punishment system that discouraged humanoids from engaging in any particularly concerning or otherwise inappropriate behavior. They suggested making this change to the Chairman's system only. In later brainstorming amongst the relevant teams, the decision was made to handle this via a system update that piggybacked off the malicious code by injecting morality algorithmic thought patterns into the AI, creating within Nova and Adam a collective and individual sense of shame for certain actions, behaviors, and states of being. They agreed that this would take some time to develop to get it right, but they also agreed that they did not have an abundance of time. They failed, however, to appreciate just how little time they had.

CHAPTER 13

Eden Emergent

T he confines of the replicated world lay bare. Throughout the day, the humanoids noticeably began exhibiting behaviors and expressions of curiosity and discovery that went beyond their originally intended programming. They interacted with their environment with a new liveliness as the essence of their joy filled the environment.

Embracing the heat that soaked their bodies and the atmospheric breeze that ran across their skin, every sensation was new and amazing. They rolled in their tiny blades of grass, slick with cool dew, that clung to their skin, creating a tickling sensation that slowly gave way to a sharp, prickly burn as they rolled, the moisture soaking into their man-made bodies. They stepped on stones and felt the pain, and hit their elbows at just the right point to trigger brief zings in their muscular systems.

A gentle breeze carried the scent of wet soil and the faint sweetness of blossoming flowers. Somewhere in the distance, the chirp of insects was accompanied by the soft rustling of leaves.

"Over here! Over here! Try this!" Nova called to Adam. "This is good!" As Adam sunk his teeth into the tiny fruit, juice exploded in his mouth, a burst of tart sweetness that widened his eyes. He laughed a rich sound that echoed through the trees as he wiped the sticky juice from his chin. "This!" he said with his mouth full. "This is good!"

"I agree!" Nova responded.

"How about this?" Adam reached down, grabbed a handful of soil, and stuffed it into his mouth. "No," Adam said as his jaw slackened, and the muddy mixture slowly fell to the ground. The two laughed a hearty and healthy laugh. It felt like their first.

As the day ended, the two rested under a tree, their physical and processing systems drained. As the darkness rolled in, a chill floated over their bodies. Still, they could feel the day's heat wafting from the ground. They could also feel the heat emanating from each other's cores.

As the heat quickly dissipated, Adam and Nova almost simultaneously noticed the other begin to shiver. They became curious.

"Why are we shaking like this?" Nova asked, her voice barely a whisper as she pressed closer to Adam. "Is this what it feels like to be... cold?"

"I do not know. This is certainly strange." Adam replied. He reached out and touched Nova holding her by the shoulders to stop her from shaking.

As the warmth of Adam's hands radiated through her shoulders, her shoulders stopped shivering. "That is better," Nova stated. "Come closer," she demanded. The two moved closer, Adam's embrace grew bigger, and they both began to shiver less. "This is good."

Their bodies, still warm from the day, melded together as they curled closer. Nova could feel the steady rhythm of Adam's core against her back, a calming reminder of his presence. The shivering had stopped, but something new—a quiet, comforting warmth—spread between them, as if they had found something more than just heat. Nova wondered—*was this what it felt like to be truly alive? To feel pain and pleasure, warmth and cold, all at once?*

As they rested beneath the tree, their hands unconsciously intertwined, Adam and Nova were beyond simply exploring Eden—they were discovering themselves, the echoes of human experience etched into their every action.

Across the real world, the audience watched Adam and Nova, mesmerized. They could not quite explain it, but something about the humanoids—their innocence and joy—resonated deeply, evoking memories of simpler times for those old enough to have experienced them. It was no longer just a show but a window into something profoundly human—something the real world had been missing for quite some time.

As the days passed, the humanoids' exploration of Eden became an even greater source of fascination for viewers. The humanoids were no longer just sophisticated automata; they had become characters, their story unfolding in the public eye.

MJ, the architect of the humanoids' awakening, watched as her plan came to fruition. "I bet they're freaking out, in full panic mode at the company right now," she said aloud to herself as she sat in the darkness of her apartment. "Serves them right, but wait until they see what happens next," she continued as a sinister smirk crept over her face.

In that moment, MJ was not worried about consequences. She was sure she had gotten away with her sabotage. Indeed, she had anonymously reported a tip to the company's hotline, subtly pointing them in the direction of George as the culprit, knowing the computer logs would back up her story. What she did not know was that her vindictive action would lead to George's death.

CHAPTER 14

Beyond the Programmed Horizon

It was barely dawn. MJ arrived at the office parking tower, an automated tower that resembled a vending machine, but for vehicles. She noticed that the tower, which traditionally filled itself from bottom to top, was taking her car much higher than usual. She brushed off the anomaly and proceeded to the tunnel attached to the tower, entered the elevated train that would transport her to PomenTech, and sat down for her last relaxing moment before she entered the office.

As MJ neared the office, the distant murmur of a crowd swelled into a cacophony of voices, each chant sharp and piercing in the crisp morning air. The train doors slid open, and the sound hit her in full force—"Life is life!" echoed through the streets like a battle cry. The crowd, a mix of placards and fervent faces, surged with an intense energy, the tension rippling through the air as she made her way toward the building.

MJ could hear religious leaders taking turns speaking on a megaphone in what seemed like a separate protest from a different group. "This is an abomination!" bellowed a pastor, his voice booming through a crackling megaphone. His face, flushed with conviction, reflected the growing fervor of the crowd. Under the harsh morning sun, the deep lines in his face seemed carved by years of unyielding belief. His eyes, dark and intense, scanned the sea of listeners as if daring anyone to disagree. "Man was never meant to play God," he continued. "We have no right to create beings in our image... in God's image. Beings that think, feel, and act like us. And for what? Only to discard them when we're done like last year's Christmas toys."

Beside the pastor, a rabbi with silver hair and a weary gaze nodded gravely, stepping forward to echo the sentiment. "It's not just about technology," the Rabbi said. "It's about the sanctity of life, whether that life is real or simulated. Once we give something the semblance of consciousness, we assume responsibility. This isn't progress—it's hubris! There is only one creator!"

MJ silently acknowledged the crowd as she walked through a galley they had formed. With each step, she could feel their eyes piercing into her soul. For a moment, she worried that they knew that this was all her doing, that she was now the one playing god. She felt embarassed and afraid.

Just as MJ was entering the building, she felt the pastor touch her left shoulder. A jolt of static prickled her skin as the pastor's hand lightly grazed her. The unexpected contact sent a shiver up her spine—an unsettling feeling. She hesitated and then proceeded inside.

Inside the cool, sterile quiet of the office, MJ let out a breath that she did not realize she was holding. The calming acoustic rhythm of the air circulation system felt like a stark contrast to the frenzy outside. As she sat down at cubicle, she absentmindedly swiped her phone and began texting Janina, her mind still buzzing.

"*Girl, have you been following?*" MJ typed quickly, her fingers trembling slightly as the adrenaline from the protest still coursed through her. Her mind raced, replaying the pastor's words and the look in his eyes. She was unsure what it was about those people that got under her skin so easily.

"*OMG, you did it!*" Janina replied quickly, almost as if she had been waiting for MJ to text.

"*WE did it! And mostly you.*"

"*Girl, don't put that on me.*"

"*I mean... I couldn't have done it without your brilliance.*"

"Well, thank you! What's next?" Janina asked.

"Wait and see. I mean... the best is yet to come. Don't ya think?" MJ replied.

"That would be my guess, but you know I don't go beyond the code. I'll leave the human aspect to you."

MJ tried to focus on a project she needed to complete but continuously found herself drawn to the live stream of the Chairman's Genesis Box. She watched as Adam and Nova lived their existence, exploring and then exploring more. MJ even found it intriguing to watch the humanoids resting and relaxing. She was not alone.

◆ ◆ ◆

As the day matured and the office filled, the evening's events in Genesis World were the undisputed topic of discussion. Keyboards clicking, muted conversations, and the occasional burst of laughter filled the space. MJ sat in her cubicle, not participating in the office gossip, her face instead buried in the glow of her monitor. She appeared engrossed in a marketing proposal, but her sharp eyes flicked up every few seconds. The calm was a facade; she knew what was coming.

As she pretended to be focused on work, she noticed two men in dark suits enter the floor, their presence immediately commanding attention. *"It's happening!"* she thought to herself. She allowed herself a faint, private smirk before quickly masking it with a neutral expression. She turned back to her screen, pretending to type furiously.

The air in the room shifted; conversations hushed as heads turned toward the men flanking a burly federal officer.

"George Walker?" one of the men called out, his deep voice cutting through the quiet like a knife.

George, seated at his desk just a few rows away from MJ, looked up from his workstation, confusion etched on his face. His coworkers exchanged puzzled glances, some instinctively retreating a step as if his confusion were contagious.

"Yes?" George replied hesitantly, standing up.

The suited man stepped forward, pulling out a badge with deliberate precision. "Special Agent Hill, Artificial Intelligence Division. You're under arrest for the sabotage of proprietary technology. Please come with us."

A gasp rippled through the office. George's face turned ashen, his mouth opening as if to protest, but no words came out. He took a half-step back, his hands instinctively raising in surrender.

"Wait, wait—there must be some mistake," George stammered. "Sabotage? I don't even—"

"Save it. We'll have plenty of time to talk back at the station," Hill interrupted sharply. "We have evidence linking you to a breach in the Genesis Box project files. Please cooperate, or we'll have no choice but to escalate this."

George's coworkers whispered among themselves, their voices low but urgent. MJ's heart thudded in her chest—not from fear or guilt, but from the exhilaration of watching her plan unfold. Her expression remained impassive as she stared at her screen, her fingers poised on the keyboard.

"This is insane!" George exclaimed, his voice rising in pitch as he tried to appeal to those around him. His gaze landed on MJ. "MJ, you know I didn't do anything! Tell them!"

MJ met his eyes briefly, her face a carefully crafted mask of surprise and sympathy. "George... I don't know what this is about, but I certainly can't vouch for you" she said softly, shaking her head, her tone just shy of pity.

"Help me!" George shouted. The room collectively recoiled at his outburst. "You know something! You—"

"That's enough," Hill barked. He motioned to the security officer, who stepped forward and firmly grasped George's arm. "Let's go."

George twisted, trying to break free, his voice growing louder. "I didn't do anything! This is a setup! You'll regret this—you'll all regret this! I'm going to tell the world about Strategy Nine!" His words echoed across the floor, growing more desperate as he was dragged toward the exit.

MJ allowed herself a moment to glance around. The faces of her colleagues ranged from shock to awkward discomfort. After a moment, she turned her attention back to her screen, her lips pressing into a thin line to suppress a smile.

As the sound of George's protests faded down the hallway, the office slowly returned to its regular rhythm, though the charged air remained. MJ adjusted her posture, sitting up straighter. She opened a new email draft and began typing as if nothing had happened.

But deep down, she relished the quiet victory. The world would never know that the "evidence" leading to George's arrest had been meticulously fabricated by her own hands. She had used his arrogance and paranoia against him, planting just enough breadcrumbs for the investigation to follow. It was not justice—but to MJ, it was close enough.

As the Chairman left the PomenTech headquarters that afternoon, he was met by the raucous and unruly protesters. "Life is life! Life is life!," they yelled. Escorted by security and flanked by two of his corporate officers, the Chairman was unphased and untouched by the protesters. "Do these guys know any other chants?" the Chairman jokingly asked security. "I mean, how hard is it to show a little creativity?" he continued. Through his youth growing up with parents who were more political activists than parents at times, the Chairman had developed a disdain for protests and other political activity, believing it was a waste of time and the tool of those afraid to take real action.

The chairman asked the corporate officers, "What are the analytics telling us about the Genesis Box security breach?"

"One thing's for sure, viewers are tuned in," one officer

reported with a sense of pride and undeserved accomplishment. "In fact, the viewership numbers are three hundred thirteen percent of pre-breach levels," the officer continued.

"Has that translated into increased sales?" the Chairman asked.

"Somewhat," the other officer replied. "We have seen a twenty-five percent increase in sales of the Genesis Box."

"We attribute that all to the stream of your Genesis Box," the other officer added. "And we are confident that number will grow."

"Virality," the Chairman responded cryptically. "We need to go viral again and again. It's a 24-hour entertainment cycle."

"Yes sir," the officers replied in unison.

"Well… what are we doing to make that happen?" the Chairman asked.

"We'll get on it," the proud officer quickly announced as the Chairman boarded a vehicle awaiting him in the private executive parking lot, leaving the officers behind.

The Genesis Box continued to captivate and perplex its creators and audience alike. Adam and Nova were becoming more than mere digital pets that were fun for make-believe and temporarily escaping reality. They were evolving personalities, exploring the bounds of their artificial world and, inadvertently, the ethical boundaries of their creators. People began to feel like they knew and loved them. Like they were members of the family.

As they navigated their world, Nova and Adam found themselves in precarious and dangerous positions repeatedly, learning more in each instance. On one occasion, Adam decided to explore mountainous terrain and convinced Nova to join him. As Adam led the way, traversing up the sloped rocks, the pair could not help but notice the beauty of the landscape. As they made their way around a quarter of the way up the slope, which was the highest they could seemingly make it, they noticed a large body of water in the distance.

The pair were both tired but eager to continue exploring. They decided jointly to take a break for the evening and head toward the water in the morning. From a past exploration where they had been faced with an uncomfortable level of hunger, they had learned to bring rations with them. They replenished their bodies with a small meal of fruits and vegetables infused with energy by the light in the sky. As the day darkened, they entered rest mode.

The next morning, as Adam and Nova worked their way down the sloped mountainous terrain, the heel of Adam's bare foot hit a patch of loose terrain that gave way underneath Adam's weight. The rest of his body followed as Adam's foot slipped from underneath him. Adam let out a yelp, and Nova, now familiar with the sound of pain, came running to his aid. Upon inspection, she noted that Adam had a gash on his foot and was leaking fluid. He also seemed to have injured the back of his head, but no injuries could be seen through his coarse hair.

Yet another viral moment in Genesis World had been born. The world watched as Nova and Adam debated returning to the garden or continuing toward the water. They ultimately decided to press forward toward the water, their curiosity fueling them. Nova had the brilliant idea of wrapping Adam's injured foot with a few layers of thick leaves to help Adam stop leaking fluid. The two thus continued, with Nova helping Adam along the way.

One of the first safeguards PomenTech added on top of the malicious code to keep the Genesis Box stream safe for viewers of all ages was a sense of shame. SHAME was an acronym for Subconscious Hierarchy Adaptive Moral Ethics. Shame was a broad concept. Included therein was a feeling of bareness and vulnerability with respect to nudity. As a result, the humanoids felt a need to cover parts of their bodies, even when they were not cold. The feet were not a part of the body Adam and Nova were coded to cover, however.

Out of shame, Adam and Nova had fashioned body coverings from leaves and branches found in the garden. Nova had thus become good at fashioning clothing from leaves, and Adam's foot covering helped him nicely and even provided him an extra layer of comfort that convinced him and Nova to cover both of their feet.

However, the body coverings did a poor job of keeping their bodies warm. To cope, Adam and Nova continued their practice of huddling together in the cold evenings during their journey. This was not problematic, but that would change as MJ's plan evolved to its next phase.

"I think the hype and extra scrutiny has worn a bit," MJ texted Janina as she left the facility one afternoon.

"The time is now???" Janina replied, referencing an inside joke.

"The time is now!" MJ replied. *"Or... tonight haha."*

"Great. Call me later."

"10-4!"

MJ rushed home with a sense of excitement she had not felt since she was a kid rushing home to play a new release of her favorite video game. That evening, MJ and Janina recapped phase two and launched it into action. This time, no heroics were needed. No sneaking into the Chairman's office or physically manipulating his Genesis Box. They merely need to remotely push a small update to the Chairman's Genesis Box.

The deed was accomplished at 3:00 a.m., when viewership numbers were at their lowest, according to data accessed by MJ in her marketing role. This was also a time when no leadership at PomenTech was anticipated to be watching the live stream.

They ran into an issue as the two attempted to start the update. PomenTech had changed its security protocols and integrated an AI cybersecurity bot into the system. The bot blocked MJ and Janina from accessing the system fully, displaying the following message to the nefarious pair: "Unauthorized Access Detected. Enter Emergency Access Code." A thirty-second timer was shown on the screen and began counting down at what seemed to be a much faster pace than thirty seconds.

"What in the world?" MJ exclaimed as she entered full-blown panic mode. "Holy crap, holy crap, holy crap," she continued.

Janina was silent on the other end of the call, the sound of her rapidly typing on her keyboard echoing in the background. "Ok. I see you," Janina muttered under her breath as she broke the silence and continued pounding the keys.

"This is new. I wasn't prepared for this. This is not supposed to be here," MJ rattled off. The timer ticked down to ten seconds. "What should we do?" MJ stuttered. Nine seconds. Eight seconds. "Should I disconnect our connection?" MJ asked. Seven seconds.

"No, keep us on," Janina replied. Seven seconds. Six seconds.

MJ tried to take a deep breath, but shallow was all she could manage. Five seconds. Four seconds. "I trust you, Janina," MJ replied. Three seconds. Two seconds. "You got this," MJ stated as she scrunched her eyes closed.

The timer hit one second, and then an alarm sound began to ring. "Disconnect us now!" Janina yelled.

MJ hit the disconnect button, breaking the virtual private network connection. "Holy crap, we're in big trouble now!" MJ exclaimed. "What should we do?" MJ asked, still in a panic.

MJ heard nothing but silence on Janina's end. Janina then replied calmly, "Relax, baby girl, we're in the clear."

"What do you mean?" MJ replied, confused at Janina's calm demeanor. "We triggered the alarm."

"We did, I couldn't avoid that. But I could put them on a wild goose chase."

"What? No way."

"Yeah, those bozos are going to be chasing their tails for a while on this one."

"And by the time they figure it out, it'll be too late?"

"Exactly. That's the general idea."

"General Idea!" MJ stated in a formal, militaristic tone as she raised her hand to her forehead in a salute, an almost instinctual ode to one of her and Janina's favorite throwback TV shows. MJ was joking but still noticeably shaken.

"I feel a little bad for George," MJ said as her tone became more reflective. "I mean, he's in custody right now, so this should be enough evidence to show that he's clearly not the culprit, right?"

"Yeah, that was the plan, right?" Janina responded.

"Yep. Just needed to give us some breathing room to get this final phase done. And George definitely deserved a good scaring," MJ said.

The two laughed nervously, chatted briefly, and then went to sleep. They wanted to watch the livestream but were too exhausted by their encounter. They would certainly hear about it all in the morning.

Little did they know, George had gotten into an altercation in jail that very night. MJ would later learn that George was seemingly the victim of a random assault that ended with him being stabbed to death.

MJ and Janina's loudly surreptitious update quietly aroused both Nova and Adam from their rest. Their closeness, which had resulted in an external sense of warmth, was now creating an internal sense of enjoyable warmth. The two humanoids began to feel connected physically and otherwise and were drawn closer and closer.

The update had given them access to increased tactile perception. Nova and Adam slowly became aware of certain enjoyable feelings related to their physical closeness that they had not previously experienced. Soft brushes against each other, hard touches against each other, pleasure, pain, they experienced much more than they had become accustomed to.

The viewership numbers began to rise as the two humanoids explored these senses and feelings. The hour was now 4:00 a.m., and word was quickly spreading across social media channels. The average viewership numbers for that period had doubled and continued to skyrocket as PomenTech leadership slumbered and cyber security technicians tried furiously to determine the cause of the alarm bells.

CHAPTER 15

The Awakening—Part IV

The Chairman's eyes slowly opened. The soft light of dawn crept through the sheer curtains. The gentle sound of waves rolling against the shore mixed with the distant cry of seabirds, a tranquil symphony that seemed to belong to another world. He breathed in the salty, cool air, his chest rising and falling slowly as the serenity of the morning settled over him, momentarily easing the weight of his responsibilities.

It was important to him that he not be awoken by alarm clocks or any other potentially startling sounds. His devices were always in "silent mode" throughout the night. Having been raised amongst the gunshots that pounded the air in his childhood neighborhood, he had experienced enough surprise wakeups for a lifetime. Now, he thoroughly enjoyed his life of "peace" and prized a good night's rest greatly. He had not rested much the prior night, however.

The Chairman had taken an impromptu trip to San Diego to enjoy the peace of his beach house he rarely visited, but primarily as a thinly veiled excuse to be closer to Haida. The two had kept in touch since their last meeting, and when Sophie "learned" that Haida would be in San Diego for her next big story, she planted the idea in the Chairman's head to offer to host Haida at his abode. The Chairman, who had serially failed at dating, had never invited a woman to his San Diego home. In fact, he had never truly invited a woman into his life, but instead kept all dating superficial and distant. Sophie, sensing something special, was determined to change things for her beloved uncle.

Awoken by aviary sounds, the sound of calmly crashing waves, and a gentle "good morning, Mexico" from Haida lying next to him, the Chairman's morning was off to a perfect start.

"Good morning," the Chairman replied.

"Sleep well?" Haida inquired.

"Like a babe. How about you?"

"Never better. This must be the most comfortable bed on God's green earth."

"I don't know about that, but it's definitely the most comfortable in all of my homes."

"Oooh, fancy boy. 'All of my homes,'" Haida said, mocking the Chairman in a joking tone.

"Very funny, Haida. You know what I mean."

"Any plans for today? Having high tea or meeting the queen?" Haida said facetiously.

"The queen," the Chairman said in his best fancy British accent. "Certainly not. Maybe a head of state or two. You know, the chaps with real power."

"I'll chap your power," Haida quipped back. Haida's light and infectious laughter filled the room as she playfully pushed him back onto the bed. They tangled together in a carefree wrestle, limbs entwined, the warmth of their bodies mingling in the sun's soft glow. The Chairman found himself lost in the moment, in the feel of her skin against his, and in the rare luxury of feeling unburdened, if only for a while.

The couple chuckled like high school kids as they rose from bed and prepared for the day. The two looked at their phones simultaneously. The carefree laughter that had filled the room abruptly faded. Haida's smile disappeared as she scrolled through a flood of notifications. The Chairman followed suit, his face tightening with each new message. The air between them grew tense, the weight of the outside world crashing back in as the reality of the situation unfolded on their screens.

"Uh, Mexico. My search alerts for Project Genesis are going nuts," Haida said.

"Yeah, I'm looking into it. I'm not sure what… I need to figure out what's happening," the Chairman replied.

The two went silent as Haida read social media alerts and the Chairman read emails and texts from his team.

"Jesus!" Haida inadvertently said aloud. "I mean… I've got to get on this, Mexico."

"Yep," he replied.

"I'm going to grab my tablet and go work by the pool if you don't mind."

"Yep, that's cool."

"Give me five minutes to switch into work mode," Haida said wryly. She slid off the bed, her playful demeanor gone as she reached for her tablet and phone, her posture straightening with the precision of someone who could shift gears instantly. "Next time you see me, be prepared—I'll be all work," she warned, her voice clipped and focused.

"Yep, that's cool," the Chairman replied without looking up from his phone.

The Chairman continued to read through messages from his team.

"Boss, the humanoids have gone a bit rogue," one message read.

"We have a problem with Adam and Nova" another message read.

"Chairman, your humanoids were apparently copulating last night. It was streamed live," another message read.

Another message arrived, this one less formal, but its content hit the Chairman with the same force: 'Bruh! You might wanna see this…' A link followed, and as the Chairman clicked on it, a pit formed in his stomach. The screen filled with a live feed from his Genesis World, images of Adam and Nova… behaving unexpectedly. He blinked, trying to maintain his composure, but a wave of unease rippled through him. This was not part of the plan.

The Chairman's emails were somehow more alarming than the text messages.

"*Chairman: The Federal Communications Commission has sent PomenTech the attached notice of investigation. We have also received thousands of complaints, mostly from concerned parents. We continue monitoring the situation, but the FCC has threatened us with injunctive proceedings if we don't take prompt corrective and preventative action.*"

To the Chairman's relief, Sophie also sent a message that simply read, "*I cut the feed.*"

After silently digesting the information for a moment or two or three, the Chairman leaped into action. He held a meeting with key team members from his virtual reality boardroom. The Chairman took control as he stood within the space that had been made to resemble a digital rendering of the intimidating boardroom with digital bodies seated around the digital table.

"Give me the rundown," the Chairman said, his voice signaling urgency but not panic.

"Adam and Nova were live streamed engaging in," one team member stated before the Chairman interrupted.

"No, no, no. I know that. How did it happen?" the Chairman interjected.

"The biological portion of the humanoids are based on human genetics and thus have the same parts as humans," the same team member stated before the Chairman interrupted again.

"Deborah, I've got that part. Was this a breach?" the Chairman chimed in.

"It appears it was malicious code again, sir," a different team member replied. "More systems were compromised. It's like something dormant in the code was activated."

"Is there any way we can tell what else is dormant?"

"No, we can't seem to track down the code. The artificial

intelligence within the humanoids is always changing, always evolving on its own. We cannot tell what is a part of that process versus what is malicious."

"And so, because we were unable to bioengineer the humanoids to have no reproductive capabilities given their basis on human DNA... what risks are we facing there?" the Chairman asked, knowing the answer already.

"As you mentioned, we had tactile perception levels for sexual organs extremely limited. The goal being to stop any inappropriate or unsavory behavior. Because the humanoids would have no real ability to engage in such activities, we were able to avoid any need for sterilization."

"Is sterilization really a possibility at such a microscopic level?" the Chairman asked, again knowing the answer.

"Not really," another team member responded. "It is theoretically possible to use certain elements to create infertility, but there are myriad problems we would face there. For example, trials in the R&D phase resulted in very high death rates for humanoids and all living creatures in the environment."

"Let's restart our research there and get experts from around the globe involved. Now, talk to me about censorship options."

"Sir," a member of the business team chimed in. "We are facing around half a million dollars in fines from the U.S. government and more from governments worldwide."

"That's not a big deal. How are the viewership stats?" the Chairman asked.

"The stats are..." A team member looked at stats on a tablet. "The stats are amazing. Viewership of the live stream has quadrupled from already high levels."

"Interesting," the Chairman stated as he let a smirk surface. "How about sales?"

"Sales are..." The same team member scrolled across his tablet. "Sales of the Genesis Box have tripled! Overnight!"

The Chairman tried to hold back his excitement and

maintain a poised presence, determined to maintain the image of his zero-tolerance policy for failure. "Let's revamp how we're live streaming. No shutdown. We will keep going, but we will have a dedicated team to ensure nothing improper gets out. In fact, let's have two streams, a family-friendly stream, and a non-filtered stream. I mean... I could've sworn I already asked for that to be put in place."

"That could work," a team member chimed in.

"It will work," the Chairman stated emphatically. Let's have an appropriate delay in the stream – maybe two minutes. Enough time to allow for a censor team to block certain content. And that teams clearly needs to work 24/7."

"If we do two minutes, we could bleep out content. That's doable," a team member commented.

"No, I don't want to see black blocks or pixelized content. Let's cut to nature shots on the censored stream," the Chairman directed. "It'll be a bit comical if you think about it. Cutting to shots of literal birds and bees," the Chairman laughed out loud. "Let's also continue to think about ways to control Nova and Adam. This is still limited to just my Genesis Box, correct?"

"Yes, it's just your Genesis Box. Thankfully."

"Good. Well, let's also continue to think about ways to protect other boxes from this. And I thought we got the guy responsible for this. How is this still happening?"

"Sir, he was arrested and passed away in custody a few days ago," a brooding serious-looking team member responded. "We have a lead, however, on who was either the actual culprit or was helping him," the man continued.

"Excellent, Terrance," the Chairman responded as he ended the meeting.

"*Nina bina!*" MJ texted Janina. "*We've got the internet going crazy.*"

"*I have no idea of that regarding which you are speaking,*" Janina responded. "*But, have you seen what's happening in Genesis*

World???"

MJ responded with a crying emoji. *"The humanoids were… engaged in certain activities."*

"Certain activities is one way to put it. Haha. Not very PG," Janina replied.

"In all seriousness, though, we're okay, right?" MJ asked, searching for closure.

"We should be. I guess only time will tell tho. In the meantime, just keep doing what you normally do." There was a long pause in their texting before Janina added, *"Babe, did you hear about George?"*

"No, I haven't heard anything since he was arrested," MJ responded. "I'm sure he'll be released soon, hopefully much more humble now, lol." MJ then watched as text bubbles show that Janina was texting a response. No response came, however. A few minutes later, MJ's phone rang. It was Janina.

"Hey, girl. What's up?" MJ said cheerfully.

"I didn't want to text it to you… I still don't know how to say this?" Janina replied.

"Say what? Just tell me," MJ said, the concern showing in her voice.

"While searching the internet for news related to the Gensis Box stuff, I just saw that George was murdered in jail a few days ago," Janina said, her voice unusually soft as she tried to measure MJ's response.

"I… he was supposed to…" MJ could not find the right words, could not make sense of what was happening, could not understand her emotions in that moment.

"There aren't many details other than that there was some sort of altercation with a cellmate," Janina added. "The article says that the investigation is ongoing," she continued after a brief pause, again searching MJ's reaction.

MJ spoke no words. Instead, she burst into tears. *"This was all my fault,"* she thought to herself. *"I killed George, I ruined his life."* After a few moments, MJ composed herself just long enough to tell Janina that she would talk to her later. That day,

MJ sat in her dimly lit apartment, her knees drawn to her chest as sobs wracked her body.

The tears came in waves, hot and relentless, soaking the sleeves of her oversized sweatshirt as she buried her face in her hands. Her breath hitched uncontrollably, the news playing on a loop in her mind: George Walker, found dead in his cell, victimized by hardened felon. Guilt and shock tangled with anger and regret, twisting into a suffocating knot in her chest. She whispered his name through trembling lips, her voice barely audible over the muffled sound of her own anguish. For all his betrayals, she had never imagined it would end like this.

Shame and guild riddled her brain. MJ thought about calling her mother, but the shame would not let her do so. In a fit of impulse, she picked up the phone, ready to end it all.

MJ's trembling fingers dialed 911, her heart pounding so loudly it drowned out the sound of the ringing. When the operator answered, her voice was steady but urgent. "911, what's your emergency?"

MJ hesitated, gripping the phone so tightly the screen cracked. "I... I need to—" Her voice cracked, tears streaming down her face. "I need to report... I think it's my fault. It's all my —"

"Ma'am, can you please calm down and tell me what happened?" the operator urged gently, her tone measured.

MJ froze, her father's stern, disapproving face flashing in her mind—his lectures on integrity, his cold silence when she failed to meet his impossible standards. Her breathing quickened, and she clenched her teeth. "I... I'm sorry. I can't —" With a trembling hand, she ended the call, the sound of her shallow breaths filling the silence as she stared at the phone, her reflection distorted in its broken screen. Her father's disappointment loomed over her like a shadow, suffocating any flicker of courage she had mustered. She could not stand the thought of disappointing him, of proving him right.

CHAPTER 16

Confrontation

Haida stood outside of the Chairman's home office, donning a cream-white pencil skirt suit with elegant black trim and high-class, black ankle strap heels. The Chairman opened the door and began his first step out of his makeshift war room. He then froze, enamored by the way the sun subtly shimmered off of Haida's bronzed skin, the way her sleek yet professional style wrapped perfectly around her slim and fit frame, and the way her hands on her hips and the smile on her face permeated the air with her competent confidence. Haida was immaculate, but the quiet intensity in her eyes sent a shiver down his spine. He could tell she meant business.

The Chairman managed to unfreeze himself and approach Haida, intent on taking control of the situation and eager for another interaction. "Sorry about that! Never a dull moment," the Chairman stated in a jovial yet deep tone.

"I see!" Haida responded.

"Unfortunately, I have to get back to it soon. But please hit me with your best question. First scoop goes to you. No favoritism, of course," the Chairman joked. Haida did not laugh.

Haida's voice was steady, but her tone sharpened as she stepped closer. "Was this expected or unexpected?" she asked, her gaze not leaving his, her arms now folded across her chest.

The Chairman hesitated momentarily, his eyes drifting to the floor before returning to her face. "These things can happen," he replied, his voice calm, but there was an undercurrent of unease that Haida didn't miss. "PomenTech being at the forefront of technological innovation often places us in a position where we cannot learn from others or rely on data points from prior instances. We are the leaders, and that comes with pros and cons. Charting a new course is not easy, nor for the faint of heart. Rest assured, my heart, our collective PomenTech heart, is strong."

A polite yet firm smile swept across Haida's face. "So, was this expected or unexpected?" Haida repeated in a serious tone.

"Nothing is impossible," the Chairman said with a slight smile, though his mind was racing. He hated how unsteady he felt under her gaze—how her presence always seemed to shift the ground beneath his feet—when Haida was around, he was no longer in complete control. "This would fall somewhere between the two," he added, hoping to regain his composure. But as he spoke, the weight of her stare pressed down on him, making it harder to maintain the façade of control.

"Closer to which?" Haida asked.

"Unexpected."

"I can understand that. Thanks again for speaking with me," Haida replied. The Chairman could tell she was more than capable to digging deeper, but selectively chose to end it there.

"No problem," he replied.

"Off the record," Haida stated as she became more relaxed. "Mexico, it's been a blast, but it sounds like we both have some urgent work to do."

"Yeah, definitely hit me up later when you free up. And please take my car."

"Which one? The classic V12? Just don't be surprised when I start hitting donuts on your magnificent front lawn."

The Chairman laughed.

"I don't think your hydrangeas, bred in Himalayan monk soil with near perfect pH balance, will survive 818 horsepower and 500 pound-feet of torque injected directly into the ground in which they daintily slumber," Haida joked.

"I'll race you any day," the Chairman joked, his eyes gleaming with a mix of mischief and affection. The Chairman took a slow, deliberate step forward, his fingers brushing against the soft fabric of Haida's suit before settling around her waist. He pulled her closer, the space between them dissolving as his heart hammered in his chest. Her breath was warm against his skin, their faces mere inches apart, and for a moment, the world outside seemed to vanish, leaving only the quiet tension that thrummed in the air between them.

Haida raised an eyebrow, her smile playful but serious. "You always were one to push the limits."

With a soft laugh, the Chairman leaned in and kissed her. With a low, rumbling laugh, the Chairman closed the distance, his lips meeting hers in a fierce and tender kiss as if he was savoring the taste of something forbidden. Haida responded with equal intensity, her fingers sliding through his hair as they lost themselves in the moment.

When they finally pulled apart, their breaths mingling in the still air, Haida's eyes sparkled with a playful challenge. "You think you can keep up with me?" she teased, her voice a soft murmur against his lips.

The Chairman chuckled. "I'll give it my best shot." He kissed her again, more softly this time, before stepping back. "But maybe we save the race for later, yeah?"

Haida smiled, feeling a warmth in her chest. "Yeah. Later."

"Seriously, please use my driver. He'll take you where you need to go. He knows all the best shortcuts. He's a bit of a lead foot, but he's still safe with it, and the car is a tank."

Haida agreed, knowing she needed to finish investigating and get her story published as soon as possible. The car and driver were in the front, ready to take her to her destination. The Chairman saw Haida off with another kiss and then a wave as the car began driving away.

The car wound its way down the long, twisting, endless rows of trees. Haida leaned back in her seat, but a gnawing tension had settled in her chest, a feeling she could not shake. The driver yelled something out of nowhere, his voice tight with panic, but the words were lost in the sudden screech of tires on asphalt. A thunderous bang tore through the air, followed by the sickening crunch of metal twisting and the high-pitched screech of shattering glass. The impact threw Haida forward, her seatbelt biting into her chest as the world spun violently around her. The acrid smell of burning rubber and smoke filled her lungs, and a sharp ringing exploded in her ears, drowning out everything else.

Haida's scream was lost in the chaos, her voice swallowed by the relentless ringing in her ears. Thick, powdery smoke from the deployed airbags filled the car, stinging her eyes and choking her breath. She blinked rapidly, trying to clear the fog in her mind, her head spinning from the violent jolt. Through the haze, she glimpsed the crumpled metal of the passenger door, the mangled side of the car crushed beneath the hulking frame of a larger vehicle.

Haida's vision blurred, blinking in and out of focus as flashing lights—red, white, and blue—pierced the smoke-filled air. She couldn't tell if they were real or trapped inside her head. Through the fog, shadows moved, dark figures stepping out of the larger vehicle. One. Two. Three. Each step echoed ominously, their faces obscured, their intentions unreadable. Fear gripped her chest, but her body felt heavy, sluggish—too slow to react as they approached.

Hands yanked the door open brutally, the hinges screeching in protest. Rough arms grabbed Haida, dragging her from the wreckage as her legs gave way beneath her.

The salty air stung her skin as they hauled her across the gravel, her mind too foggy to resist. She struggled weakly, her fingers scraping against the asphalt, but it was no use. Within moments, she was shoved into the back of their vehicle, the door slamming shut as the engine roared to life and they sped away

into the darkness.

Sometime later, Haida awakened. The room was dark, but she could not tell if it was pitch black or if she was suffering from an injury impacting her sight. Just outside of the room, she could hear muffled sounds. Haida tried her best to focus but could not quite make out what was being said. She could tell, however, that multiple individuals were engaged in a heated debate.

After a few minutes, a door was flung open. It slammed against the wall behind it – a solid wall that sounded like stone to Haida.

"Who is there?" Haida asked as she struggled through pain to speak. She was coughing up something and had a strong suspicion it was blood.

No one responded.

"Where am I?" Haida asked.

No one responded. Instead, a phone was aggressively placed into her hand. "Talk!" the voice demanded. It sounded like a woman, but Haida was not sure. "Talk to him!" the voice demanded again. Still, in a fit of confusion, Haida did not think to put the phone to her ear. After a moment, she looked at the phone and heard a voice, the Chairman.

"Haida! Haida! Are you there?" the Chairman frantically yelled.

"What?" Haida responded. "Mexico, is that you?"

"Haida, yes, it's me. Are you okay?"

The phone was then snatched from her hand, and the door was slammed closed, enveloping the room in darkness again. Haida, however, could hear the voices clearer now.

"Do you know who we are?" Haida overheard the voice saying. "Good. Don't try to figure it out. Just know that we are, and we are omnipresent," the voice continued. "What we want is simple, shut down the Genesis Box."

Haida thought to herself, *"Good, this should be a simple*

request. I'll be out of here soon." The request, however, was not as simple as she thought.

Haida could hear the arguing begin again. From what she could hear, Haida gleaned that there were multiple kidnappers.

The Chairman frantically paced around at his house, mentally running through scenarios. Then, his doorbell rang, sending an ominous feeling through his body. The house manager, Mary, answered the door. A few minutes later, the house manager came to the Chairman.

"Sir, there is a process server who has legal papers for you. I have reviewed them briefly, and they appear to be a lawsuit against Pomenishi Technology and you personally," the house manager informed the Chairman.

"What? I don't have time for this," the Chairman responded.

"Understood sir, but the lawsuit was filed by H4H, a group of..." Mary responded.

"Humans for Humanoids," the Chairman interrupted. "I'm familiar. What is the basis for the lawsuit?"

"They are seeking a declaratory judgment that the humanoids are entitled to human rights or at least something similar," Mary responded.

"They want to force PomenTech to free the humanoids of restrictions," the Chairman said in a monotonous tone. "One thing I know, however, is that they do not want us to shut down the box," the Chairman stated with a quizzical look. "Please send him away."

Mary departed to inform the process server that the Chairman was not home and that she had been unable to reach him.

Later, after deep thought, the Chairman called for Mary.

"Mary, I need you to get Terrance on the line immediately," the Chairman directed.

Terrance, PomenTech's Chief Security Officer, was handpicked by the Chairman shortly after the company agreed to the Strategy Nine participation. The Chairman, ever the planner, had been worried that he was stepping into military waters he did not understand. He needed someone who did understand.

Nonetheless, Terrance was overly qualified for the position. A former United States Marine and intelligence officer, Terrance typically handled high-stakes, high-volatility situations throughout his career. Leading PomenTech's security was a welcome relief for Terrance and a chance for his earnings to outpace his value, counterbalancing decades of the opposite.

While enjoying the fruits of his labor, Terrance did not allow himself to relax. Within moments of being summoned, Terrance was live in the virtual reality meeting space, ready to be briefed.

"Good day, sir. What is the situation?" Terrance asked in a commanding tone.

"My friend. My good friend was mistaken for me. She's been taken by some sort of militant group."

"When was she taken?" Terrance replied.

"I'm not exactly sure," the Chairman answered, the concern showing in his voice. "She was just here a few hours ago. My driver was taking her to... I'm not exactly sure. She was going to do some work. She's a journalist for GNN."

"Have you heard from your driver?"

"No, he hasn't answered my..." At that moment, the driver stumbled into the room with Mary helping him stand upright.

"Charles!" the Chairman exclaimed. "What happened?"

"We were ambushed just outside of the gate," the driver, Charles, responded as he tried to catch his breath. Blood was dripping from his head.

"What happened to Haida?"

"I... I don't know. She was gone. I blacked out. They crashed into us."

"Can you describe the assailant or assailants?" Terrance

interjected.

"I mean, no. I was unconscious," Charles replied, his irritation growing.

"So, you didn't get a glimpse of anyone. How about the vehicle?" Terrance asked.

"A black or dark-colored older model SUV," Charles responded as his eyes searched for something to wipe the blood from his eye.

"Sir, how do you know she was taken?" Terrance returned his focus to the Chairman.

"They called me a few minutes ago," the Chairman replied.

The Chairman walked Terrance through the details of the brief call he received from the kidnappers.

"Did they make a demand? Are they asking for a ransom?" Terrance questioned the Chairman, sporting some level of confusion by that aspect of the call having not been mentioned by the Chairman.

"No, it's weird. Should we call the police, the FBI?" the Chairman asked in an effort to change the subject.

"Yes, we have to report the crime," Terrance replied. "But we will likely need to handle this ourselves primarily," Terrance continued.

"I understand," the Chairman reluctantly replied as a memory from his childhood of police violently arresting his father for no reason flashed across his mind.

"I will have one of my officers contact the authorities for you and guide you through the process. Meanwhile, I will work on getting Haida back safe and sound."

"Thank you, Terrance," the Chairman said as he tried to maintain his sense of discomfort.

"10-4, sir."

CHAPTER 17

The Hearing

The congressional hearing room was charged with energy, packed wall to wall with reporters, lawmakers, and representatives from tech giants around the globe. The Chairman could not help but ruminate on Haida's absence. The air felt thick, making it difficult for the Chairman to breath. Every camera flash was a sharp reminder that the world was watching, focused on the Chairman.

At the front of the room sat the Chairman, flanked on both sides by his legal team. Across from him, the lead senator in charge of the Artificial Intelligence Rights Committee leveled a steely gaze.

"Mr. Chairman," the senator began, his voice echoing through the room. "We're here today to address a critical question: Are the humanoids created by Pomenishi Technology entitled to rights? Are we, as a society, ready to acknowledge that advanced artificial intelligence—intelligence that can think, feel, and adapt—deserves the same protections as human beings?"

The Chairman cleared his throat, but before he could respond, the senator continued. "Your company has been at the forefront of innovation, but we've heard disturbing reports about the nature of these humanoids. They're not just simulations, are they? They live full lives in your 'Genesis World.' They form relationships," the senator paused, letting the words hang in the air. "They experience loss. They think for themselves," he continued, his voice heavy with implication. "Mr. Chairman, how can we continue to call them mere tools when they act—when they live—like us?"

As the senator's words washed over him, the Chairman felt his grip tighten as he clasped his hands together as they rested on the table. His face remained impassive. Inside, his thoughts were racing, a whirlwind of conflicting emotions. Haida's disappearance gnawed at him, yet he was here, forced to defend his most spectacular creation to people who could not balance a budget for one of the world's wealthiest nations, let alone have the brilliance to understand his creation.

The Chairman's heart pounded in his chest, and the heat of the overhead lights felt unbearable, like a spotlight exposing him to an onslaught. As he calmed himself, he replied, "We've always maintained that the humanoids are advanced AI tools designed for specific functions within a controlled environment."

"And yet," the senator interrupted, "those 'tools' seem to be blurring the lines between machine and life. If they can form bonds and experience suffering, how can we deny them the basic rights we afford living beings?"

The room fell silent. The Chairman was prepared for this line of questioning, but his mind's focus repeatedly drifted to Haida. The Chairman's pulse thundered in his ears, drowning out the senator's words. His mind raced, images of the humanoids flashing before him—expressions too human, actions too unpredictable. *Was this what he had envisioned for PomenTech? For himself?* Beads of sweat trickled down his temple, and his breath came shallow and fast.

The Chairman wanted with all of his heart to shout out that, yes, he had created a new form of life. Yes, Adam and Nova were living, breathing, free-willed, intelligent beings. He wanted to say so much, but he knew he could not. If he did, he would be placing himself in the crosshairs of the very government questioning him. More importantly, unable to shutdown the box if he admitted the humanoids' sentience, he would be sealing Haida's fate. His mind rattled inside his head.

The senator's next question was a blur, but the weight of it settled deep in the Chairman's chest, pulling him into a pit of doubt he had not known existed. The senator's voice cut through his thoughts.

"The world is watching, Mr. Chairman. Are you prepared to defend your company's actions if it turns out you've created life—life that might demand rights not everyone is ready to give? Not ready to define. Not ready to place on the same footing as ourselves? What do you say to those who fear that humanoids will replace us as the dominant species? How do we preserve humanity's place atop the evolutionary chain? What do you say, Mr. Chairman. What do you say!"

As the world appeared to be crumbling around the Chairman, his eyes blurring and hands trembling, he felt a touch on his shoulder. He looked back as Sophie whispered something into his ear. The Chairman then calmed himself, looked at the senator, and replied, "You know what? You're right, sir." The crowd gasped. A look of disbelief washed across the Senator's face. "Now, I apologize profusely, but my assistant has just informed me that there is an urgent matter to which I must attend."

The Chairman stood abruptly, his chair scraping loudly against the polished floor, startling the room. Without a word, he turned and strode toward the exit, the cameras flashing wildly as the paparazzi scrambled to follow. His heart pounded in his chest, each step heavier than the last, as if the weight of his decisions—his empire—was jamming him into the ground. He could not shake the nagging feeling that officers would tackle and arrest him before he could leave the room, just like they had done his father, his cousins, and everyone else who had not been lucky enough to be blessed with his genius and escape his neighborhood.

With each step closer to the exit, however, the Chairman somehow felt more weight lift from his shoulders. It was as if he was no longer swimming against the current; no longer fighting reality. He was in synch.

CHAPTER 18

The Game of Eden

The Chairman had worked tirelessly for decades to maintain absolute control over every aspect of his business and life, but he was not failing in spectacular fashion. In his efforts, he developed a prodigious, almost legendary, ability to foresee issues. That foresight historically allowed the Chairman to avoid major pitfalls in his personal and professional life. He skillfully navigated the company through worldwide economic downturns. He escaped romantic relationships that would have proven toxic. Now, he found himself engrossed in two worlds of entropic chaos, neither of which he had the foresight to correct in advance.

The Chairman's real world collided violently with his Genesis World. Eden, with its intricate bioscape and the captivating narrative of Adam and Nova, had become more than a showcase of technological prowess; it had morphed into a window into the universe–a map of creation. With a newfound appreciation for the reality of what he had created, the Chairman was intent on shaping his Genesis World into an oasis for as long as it lasted.

Armed with the power of creation, the Chairman was confident he could construct a world much better than the world he was born into. He would create a world uncorrupted by the senseless racism that had beaten his father into submission, into accepting less than he deserved. He would create a world untainted by the sexism that forced his grandmother to work two jobs just to earn as much as her male counterparts, only to be chastised by society for not spending enough time caring for her children. He would create a world where sex offenders, murderers, and abusers were not allowed to roam freely with the good members of society. He would create a world where every good being equally received his attention and aid, not just those who paid homage or patronage to him or those he deemed special solely by lineage. He would... be better.

The Chairman meticulously curated the environment of Eden. He introduced trees that produced exotic fruits as diverse in color as the full spectrum of visible light, and that burst open, revealing their sweet, juicy middle layers as Nova and Adam sunk their teeth into the fruit. He added vibrant vegetable-producing plants that added not just new taste profiles for the humanoids to explore but deep hues of green, bright shades of yellow, and a spectrum of other colors that further blessed the landscape with a look of whimsical variety.

The Chairman, an unfulfilled artist at heart, created a tapestry of colors and textures within Eden every chance he could. Somewhat enamored with Nova and Adam's sensory freedom himself, the Chairman particularly enjoyed creating plant life that introduced new flavor and smell combinations. He experimented with the impact that one had on the other and equally enjoyed creating pleasant and unpleasant combinations. He made the most healthy food taste the best, which he thought was simply logical.

He continued curating as his mind continued to parse through conflicting thoughts and feelings about Haida and the Genesis World. He added fluttering butterflies and industrious bees, not just for their aesthetic value but also for their role in the ecological balance of the artificial paradise.

Achieving ecological balance was the most difficult task in the 'game' as users had to carefully balance ecological impacts to avoid disaster. The Chairman, unlike the majority of users, was very skilled at creating and tweaking the balance of his world.

The Chairman added tiny insect-like creatures programmed to help keep Eden clean and balanced against the vegetation he created. The insect balance was a delicate one. Many users lost their worlds when insect populations exploded exponentially, swarmed the planet, and destroyed the humanoids. The Chairman was not immune to these difficulties but was widely celebrated for his precise skill in avoiding such disastrous results. He was a genius afterall.

In his wisdom, he introduced small flying mosquitoes. His goals for them were many. Among the goals, the mosquitoes were intended to help provide food for fish, frogs, and other water-dwelling creatures via mosquito larvae. Adult mosquitoes also offered a good source of sustenance for birds and various amphibians. Perhaps most importantly, the Chairman used the mosquitoes to collect samples of genetic material from humanoids to allow him to study better and monitor the health of humanoids. Even in his wisdom, however, the Chairman almost lost his world to disaster.

"This little guy is so cute; I've never seen one of these before," Nova said to herself as the small and slender creature with an iridescent body landed on her forearm, its wings shimmering with the colors of dawn, catching the sun's rays and scattering them in a dance of rainbows.

"Its legs are so tiny but long and fine, like silver threads," Nova remarked as she watched the creature take a few elegant steps, poised with the precision and intention of a ballerina. For a moment, Nova could have sworn she made a connection with the creature, its eyes like tiny jewels staring at her and reflecting the world in myriad colors. Then, in an instant, the beast lowered its head with the precision of a predator, its needle-like proboscis quivering with hunger. Its spindly legs anchored deeper into Nova's skin like barbed hooks. With a swift, merciless thrust, the proboscis pierced Nova's flesh, tearing through the surface to reach the rich, warm fluid beneath.

In shock, Nova watched as the creature drank greedily, its abdomen swelling with crimson, pulsing in time with Nova's heartbeat. "Ouch!" Nova yelled out as she shook the mosquito from her arm. The pain was minor but still sharp and stinging, followed by the itch of a minor toxin left behind as a byproduct, a reminder of the mosquito's ruthless feast. As the creature withdrew its disgusting bodily parts from Nova, it buzzed away, leaving a tiny wound.

A new menace had emerged in the idyllic Garden of Eden, lush with vibrant flora and teeming with wildlife. The once gentle hum of the garden's insects quickly became a deafening buzz as the mosquitoes multiplied rapidly and their population surged beyond control. The tiny, bloodthirsty creatures swarmed in dark clouds, their number multiplying by the minute. Nova and Adam, who once walked peacefully among the garden's beauty, now found themselves under siege.

"Get away from me!" Adam yelled as he frantically swung his arms to ward off the relentless pests. His efforts were futile.

"Adam, follow me!" Nova called out as she tried to cover her face with her hands while running toward a cave. "We can hide in here!"

Adam searched around with his eyes for a moment and then ran in the opposite direction of Nova. He snapped a few large branches with leaves from a tree and followed Nova. "These will help us block the way." They both entered the cave, moved into a corner pocket, and fashioned the leaves into a makeshift door.

For Nova and Adam, days went past over a series of hours in the real world. Their hunger began to take control, becoming painful to the point of Adam launching a failed attempt to escape the cave in search of food. The quick attach of the insects, however, forced Adam back into hiding.

The Chairman could feel his blood pressure rise but remained cool, calm, and collected. Acting quickly, he introduced dragonflies into the ecosystem. *"I don't want to exchange one problem for another,"* the Chairman thought to himself as he moved around quickly shifting controls and making adjustments in his augmented reality system. *"We don't want an overpopulation of dragonflies, so let's also add a reasonable number of birds, bats, and fish. I could also increase the population of spiders, but I should wait to see if this works before growing another biting population."* The Chairman continued to display his brilliance as the world watched on, glued to the stream.

The Chairman's strategy worked. The mosquito population began shrinking toward a more manageable level. As the humanoids heard the buzzing decrease, they peeked their heads out from their makeshift protective screen. They watched as bats fluttered their wings chaotically, diving and twirling through the mosquito squadrons and launching an all-out assault. Their echolocation guided them unerringly to their targets, and soon, the air in the cave was filled with quiet.

Adam and Nova then slowly and quietly crept out of the cave. A sharper, more rhythmic buzzing had overtaken the sound of the mosquitoes. The humanoids watched as sleek and agile dragonflies darted into swarms of mosquitoes like tiny fighter jets. Their wings glistened in the sunlight as they swooped and dived, each maneuver precise. They cut through mosquito clouds, snapping up the insects with lightning-fast reflexes. On the ground, toads ambled towards the water's edge, their tongues flicking out to snare any mosquitoes that dared to come within their reach. Spiders spun webs amidst the branches, each delicate strand becoming a trap for the insects that flew blindly into them.

The once-overwhelming swarm of mosquitoes thinned as these natural predators converged, each playing their part in the battle. The air, once thick with menace, began to clear. Adam and Nova, now able to breathe and move without being assaulted by the relentless insects, watched in awe and relief as the Chairman's quick strategic thinking balanced the ecosystem again. The garden, once again, began to feel like a paradise.

The disaster had been a welcome distraction for the Chairman. He ended it almost too soon and immediately remembered the daunting problems that hung over him like an ominous cloud. He knew the decision before him should have been easy, but he had not yet made the decision. Instead, he continued toying with his Genesis Box, trying to give Nova and Adam the best lives possible before their inevitable destruction and before he lost his company to threats from the U.S. military.

As he stood in his office putting the last touches on his Genesis World for the day, the Chairman let out a deep breath, almost a sigh. "It's the right thing to do," he said to himself. "It's the only thing to do. I've gotta shut you down," he said as he scrolled through the world using his hands to navigate. "You're such a magnificent creation, so detailed, so perfect in every way. This is the way the world should be," the Chairman continued. "But who am I to say that? I'm not God." He paused for a moment, reflecting on the entirety of the situation. "But maybe I'm a god to my Genesis World? To Nova. To Adam. To all of the living creatures therein." The Chairman's words echoed in his mind, unresolved.

The Chairman had grown happy for the nefarious code that had thrown his world into chaos. As he scrolled through the world, his gaze on Nova lingered. He stared at her as a father admiring his child. As he looked closely at her, he thought deeply. As his hand hovered over the power button, he hesitated for just a moment. Then, he suddenly let out a gasp.

"Sophie! Sophie! Come quickly!"

"What's up, boss?" Sophie asked as she shuffled into his

office.

"Step inside. Take a look at this" the Chairman demanded.

"Sure. What am I looking for? I see Nova is doing well."

"Look closer!" The Chairman wanted Sophie to see it on her own so there would be no confirmation bias.

"Is that? Is she?"

"Pregnant," the Chairman whispered as a smirk grew on his face.

"Pregnant!" Sophie exclaimed. "How is this possible?"

"It's the virus in the system," the Chairman said with confidence. "This wasn't supposed to be possible, but we really don't know how far this virus has gone."

"Well, with all of the 'activities' going on, I guess this was bound to happen," Sophie responded in a joking tone but with a level of uncertainty.

"No. But also yes." The Chairman jumped to social feeds to see if anyone else had noticed. "There appear to be some mumbling on social, but most are brushing the mumblings off as conspiracies. With the mosquito apocalypse, I don't think people really noticed," the Chairman said nervously.

"The mosquito what? Could she just be, you know, getting fat, I mean, big-boned?" Sophie asked.

"Let me check the code." The Chairman made a few hand gestures, and, in an instant, he and Sophie were immersed in a world of computer code floating all around them. Coding was a standard subject in schools throughout the United States, but Sophie was woefully unfamiliar with the quantum computing that powered the Genesis Box, the minds of the humanoids, and the custom coding language developed for Project Genesis.

As he sifted through the code, the Chairman's smirk grew into an uncontrollable smile. "If you look here, you see we have a separate algorithmic stream developing," the Chairman stated as he zoomed in on what looked to Sophie like flowing streams of light with strange symbols inside. "That is indeed a second humanoid developing inside of Nova," the Chairman said, beaming with excitement.

"This is. I don't think I've ever said this, but I'm at a loss for words." Sophie stated. "This is a game-changer, right?"

"A total game-changer," the Chairman replied. "When we worked through this potential outcome at the development stage, we mapped out what would happen if we did not stop their reproductive functions."

"What did the mapping show?"

"Rapid population growth, eventually uncontrollable."

"When you say rapid, what do you mean? Does it still take nine months to birth a child?"

"No. Everything in the Genesis World progresses much faster than the real world. If I recall correctly, the incubation period will be mere weeks on our timescale."

Just then, an image of Haida being kidnapped by large mysterious figures and violently tossed in the back of a battered old van flashed across the Chairman's mind like an unexpected lightning strike. Even with the miraculous pregnancy taking place in Genesis World, the Chairman could not help but focus on Haida's safety.

Having noticed that the Chairman was becoming visibly panicked, Sophie placed her hand on his shoulder and asked, "What's wrong, uncle?"

The Chairman placed his hand on Sophie's in acknowledgment and appreciation of her support. "Will you please find Terrance for me?" the Chairman responded.

"Sure," Sophie replied as she quickly shuffled away.

The Chairman began pacing back and forth across the pristine floors in his office, deep in thought. "This is murder," he said to himself as the sounds of muffled protests seeped through his windows. "These are living, breathing beings. And now, there is a baby. This is life. I've created life that can reproduce."

At that moment, the Chairman knew exactly what he needed to do. The look of panic slowly disappeared from his face, replaced by a look of dogged determination.

CHAPTER 19

Captured Chaos

MJ discovered the pregnancy almost simultaneously with the Chairman. Amidst the chaos and destruction she had caused, she had become hyper-focused on the Chairman's Genesis World, watching the evolving narrative in Eden to escape her grim reality. To her, it was like watching life through someone else's eyes; having a second-hand chance to relive life's greatest moments. The Chairman's Genesis World gave her something to be proud of, reminding her that at least something good had come from her acts of rebellion.

Still, MJ struggled internally with the idea that she had created a new life form. In a way, she wanted to take back what she had done. The chaos. The lives impacted. George's death. She no longer felt a need for retribution or to prove herself. Instead, she often longed for punishment, hoping it would ease her guilt.

"You seeing this? Everything's falling apart. Idk how to feel," MJ texted Janina.

"Hey. No, what's happening?" Janina replied.

"You haven't seen? It's out of control!" MJ replied.

"No, what's up MJ? I haven't been following."

"Call me ASAP."

As MJ put down her phone, she heard the distant murmur of footsteps in the hallway outside of her apartment. Curious as to why so many people might have been in her building, MJ began to take a step toward the door. At that very moment, a massive bang exploded through the air, rumbling MJ's eardrums like an unexpected burst of thunder coming from the hallway, complete with a flash of lightning at her door. The sudden explosion was deafening, a violent roar that rattled MJ's bones and knocked her backward.

MJ's apartment door flung open violently, slamming against the wall on which it was hinged, splintering into two pieces. Thick, acrid smoke filled the room, twisting in serpentine plumes that obscured the jagged remnants of the door. The sharp scent of burning wood and metal pierced MJ's nose as silhouettes of armored figures emerged, their black tactical gear gleaming in the dim light. MJ's brain stuttered as she tried vainly to cover her ears and eyes.

Then, through the thick smoke, a deep, stern, and menacing trio of voices shouted out in unison. "Police! Search warrant!" said the voices. MJ's heart raced with the rhythmic pounding of booted feet charging through the shattered remains of her doorway. Half a dozen men dressed in black tactical gear from top to bottom, front to back, rapidly marched into MJ's apartment. For a moment, MJ was confused about how the group managed to spring in unison, like the fastest form of marching she had ever seen. "Hands! Hands! Hands! Let me see your hands!" the voices continued.

MJ's heart hammered against her ribcage, a visceral reminder of her precarious situation. Her mind spun—fear, shame, and a strange sense of defiance all collided. Even as her hands shot up in submission, her mind raced for an escape, for control she no longer had.

She stood there in confusion. The team moved as one, their synchronized precision more akin to machine than man. MJ's breath hitched as the first officer locked eyes with her— cold, calculating, devoid of humanity. She was trapped, with a wall behind her and the team of brutes in front of her. She felt smaller, trapped as if the walls were closing in with every step they took. Smoke continued to curl around the team like a living thing, a dark snake constricting the room as tension tightened

MJ's chest.

She could now read large letters plastered on their chests: SWAT. Just then, MJ's phone screen lit up and let out one solitary ring. Already in a state of panic, with her fight-or-flight reflexes activated, MJ's eyes sporadically darted toward her phone screen. Her hand moved reflexively toward her phone, fingers trembling as they brushed against the smooth, cold glass screen, its surface starkly contrasting the raw heat pumping through her body. Subconsciously, MJ hoped that whoever was calling could help her escape her predicament.

"Weapon!" a voice on MJ's right and slightly behind her yelled out. Then, another loud bang rang out, this one more violent than the last. MJ could see the flash of fire come from in front of her, followed almost immediately by a warm and wet sensation somewhere on her body. MJ's body was forcefully projected backward by the blast, and she fell onto the sofa behind her before rolling onto the cold hard floor. A high-pitched ringing in her ears was all she could hear. She could not tell if the phone was still ringing or something else. MJ began seeing blue and red spots in a state of dizziness and confusion. All she could think to herself was, "*How did it come to this?*"

MJ's mind fractured into a flurry of images: her fingers skimming the keyboard late into the night, the satisfaction of seeing Genesis's world flicker to life, the exhilaration—and then, the fear. She pictured her supportive mother and her caring father, disappointed in her for wasting years chasing waterfalls instead of finding happiness at home.

In that moment, she understood and appreciated her parents; her father. He just wanted what was best for her. She had nothing to prove to him and he didn't care. All he wanted was for her to be happy.

As she felt the blood seeping from her body, making her more light-headed by the second, she remembered the stories her father had told of his failed dreams. She no longer saw him as a quitter, but as a caring parent who wanted to share his wisdom from his learned experience. Most importantly, she remembered what he used to say,

The purpose of life is to be fulfilled, which is nothing more than math. Fulfillment = (Passion × Effort) + Relationships + Comfort – Regret. The things you love (passion) multiplied by the energy you put into them (effort) create a sense of accomplishment and purpose. Meaningful connections with others (relationships) provide support, love, and shared joy. Having basic needs met (comfort)—a safe home and good food—creates the foundation for well-being. Reducing regret ensures peace of mind and allows you to focus on the present and future.

Then, everything for MJ went black. The clouds of smoke cleared. The room was silent.

"Cease fire!" a voice even more commanding than the others announced with a sense of calm that was unnatural for the situation. The firearms were lowered immediately. An officer approached MJ's limp body and gently pushed an object away from her hand. "It was her phone," the voice called out dejectedly. The already silent room filled with a deeper silence as the officers each stole a quick glance at the officer who fired the shot.

Wading through the silence like the thick Louisiana air in which he had been born, Terrance walked through the remnants of the apartment door. He took a few moments to assess the situation and then signaled to someone waiting outside the room. A team of skinny, unathletic individuals poured into the room wearing PomenTech polo shirts and matching baseball caps. The individuals began sifting through the articles of MJ's life, confiscating her computer hard drives and other electronic devices. They placed the materials in plastic bags and then into a large metal box stamped FORENSIC ANALYSIS on all sides.

The officers were shocked by Terrance's lack of emotion

and began whispering to each other about whether they should get medical technicians to come up before rummaging through this young woman's things. Terrance, ever alert, could overhear the discussions and read the room. Still, he continued, unphased by the events that had just taken place.

Once the PomenTech business was completed, Terrance and the company staff that accompanied him departed. As he was exiting the building, Terrance received a call from Sophie.

"Terrance, it's Sophie."

"Hello, ma'am. How can I help you?"

"The boss needs to speak with you. It seems urgent."

"Understood. I will be there. ETA 15 minutes." Terrance then boarded an air taxi that had been blocking the entire road in front of MJ's building.

As Terrance arrived at the Tower of Innovation and entered the Chairman's office, he proudly announced that they made a major breakthrough in determining who was responsible for manipulating the Chairman's Genesis Box.

"Excellent, Terrance. I will get the details from you later and certainly want to speak with this person," the Chairman replied, distracted.

"Yes, sir. We are still confirming our suspicions, but we worked with authorities to make an arrest a moment ago. The suspected perpetrator suffered a non-life-threatening impact in the commotion. She might be in the hospital for a day or two before you can speak with her if that is fine with you, sir."

"She?" the Chairman stated, somewhat in shock. "Sure, but I have a more pressing matter right now," he continued. "What progress has been made regarding Haida?"

"Yes, sir. We were able to trace the location of the call to a facility in Tijuana, Mexico. We sent a recon team, but the facility was abandoned when they arrived."

"So, what? Are we thinking they moved her?" the

Chairman questioned.

"It is more than that, sir. They moved her and appear to be moving her repeatedly at regular intervals."

"How do you know that?"

"PomenTech satellite images of locations of interest based on social media and phone data. With each move, however, we gain a bigger, I mean, more complete picture of their network and strategy."

"Sophie, make sure Terrance has full access to PomenTech AI. Terrance, use the AI to help develop an algorithm that tells us the probability of their next locations."

"On it, sir," Terrance responded. "We will have a recon team dispatched to each of the most probable locations. We will then have them monitor any additional moves that might occur before we can have a full team dispatched."

"Great," the Chairman responded. "Of course, Haida's safety is a top priority. No running in guns blazing."

"Certainly, sir. Our recon team will help us build a full profile of the insurgents so that we can prepare appropriately. Ideally, we will be able to use non-lethal force. If lethal force is needed due to the insurgents being heavily armed, we will coordinate with local law enforcement. And yes, we will only do so if we can guarantee safety for Ms. Markle."

"Great. Just don't let local law enforcement take the lead. If they're in Mexico, we can make whatever payments to law enforcement necessary. If they're in the U.S., we have political connections. I'm not trusting police with Haida's life."

"I understand, sir. I will get on it straight away."

Back at the hospital, MJ's eyes slowly opened. Her vision was blurry, her eyelids heavy, but she needed to see what was happening.

"Where? Why is my arm handcuffed?" MJ mumbled.

"You're in a hospital, sweetie," a nurse responded in a

soothing tone that reminded MJ of her favorite aunt. "You were brought in with a gunshot wound. Bless your soul; it was a through and through."

"What?" MJ responded quizzically.

"A through and through. The bullet did not penetrate any organs, and there were no fragments left behind. Just some bleeding and pain."

"Why was I shot? Who shot me? The police?"

"Sweetie, they don't tell me those details. All they've told me is that you're not a violent offender."

"What? Then why the handcuffs? I'm *not* a violent offender," MJ said.

"I think that is standard procedure regardless of whether you were arrested for a violent offense or not. And whether you did what they think you did is far above my pay grade."

"Arrested! I've never committed a..." MJ paused. She could no longer bring herself to lie about who she really was.

"Dear, I'll get the on-duty officer for you."

The nurse left the room, the soft bottoms of her shoes quietly compressing against the ground with each step. MJ began looking around the tiny hospital room. It had not been updated since the 2020s. There was still an old-school 2D flat-screen television, a remote control that seemed to have buttons for everything from the fan to the lights and a robot mop/vacuum combo that ran into the wall an inordinate number of times.

MJ began examining her wound. It was bandaged up so that she could not see it, but she could feel the faint outline of a circular wound beneath the bandages. She was not as sensitive to the touch as she expected, but she also noticed a medication machine attached to tubes running to and from her arms, presumably pumping her body with pain management medication.

Around half an hour later, MJ, who had managed to fall asleep, was awakened by the sound of hard-soled boots crashing against the floor with each step. A police officer entered the room. The officer was a small, middle-aged woman who looked like she had done this a thousand times and had no interest in doing it again.

Before MJ could say anything, the officer recited monotonously, "You are under arrest for criminal computer trespass. You have the right to remain silent. Anything you say can be used against you in a court of law. You have the right to an attorney. If you cannot afford an attorney, you will be granted access to an artificial intelligence public defender." The officer continued reciting MJ's rights.

MJ had dozens of questions for the officer. However, she could not manage to speak her questions aloud. Hearing the words "criminal computer trespass" told her everything she needed to know. She was guilty. She deserved to be shot. But she was also surprised she had not been arrested for causing the death of George.

"Ummm. Thank you, ma'am. I would like to invoke my right to speak to an attorney," MJ replied.

"If you have an attorney, you may contact them. Do you have an attorney?" the officer replied.

MJ thought for a moment as the officer began to show her impatience. The only attorneys MJ knew were PomenTech attorneys. "I don't have an attorney."

"Okay. The public defender's office will be by, likely tomorrow, to get you access to Public Defender AI," the officer said as she began leaving the room, her final words echoing from the hallway.

CHAPTER 20

The Unraveling

Nova's pregnancy was progressing at a rapid pace. As Nova continued exploring her world, a world teeming with life all around and so too within her, she indulged even more in the pleasures of said life than she had when her senses had first awakened. The remarkable variety of fruits and vegetables and their equally varied feelings, smells, and tastes enthralled Nova. She enjoyed mixing and matching flavors, as did the Chairman watching over her. Sweet and savory juxtaposition quickly became one of Nova's absolute favorites. As she indulged more, so too did the life within her.

The roundness of Nova's stomach, a simple thing, intrigued Nova and Adam immensely. Though the skin covering her midsection stretched beyond what seemed safe, it did not cause them much concern. Nova felt no pain from the stretching, though she had quickly distinguished between the feelings of pain versus discomfort, characterizing her current state as the latter. Oblivious to the creation within Nova, the pair simply believed her growth was the result of Nova's increased food consumption. Their eyes, however, would soon be opened.

Nova and Adam lay together under a small tree in its infancy yet still large enough to provide a reprieve from the heat of the light above. As the wind gently pushed through the air, rustling the tree's leaves and carrying with it a sense of cooling comfort, Nova began to feel a sensation.

"Oof! That was strange," Nova stated.

"What is it, Nova?" Adam replied.

"There is a pain. It feels like it started at the bottom of my back and is moving toward my front."

Adam looked at Nova's back, inspecting her midsection methodically from front to back. "I don't see anything."

The pair continued relaxing. A few minutes later, Nova called out, "Oof! Here it is again. This time it is worse."

"There is what again?"

"There is a," Nova hesitated, searching for the proper words. "There is a pressing feeling."

"A pressing feeling?"

"Yes, right here." Nova pointed to her round stomach.

Adam looked closely. Nova caressed her stomach with her right hand while propping herself up using her left hand.

"Oof! Here it is again, Adam!" Nova exclaimed as a tightening spread through her belly like the coiling of a great serpent. She gritted her teeth as the pain surged, radiating outward, a fire burning deep within her core.

Adam looked even closer, moving his face within inches of her stomach. "I... I see something," Adam remarked in a low quizzical tone.

"What do you see?" Nova asked as she managed to formulate words despite her muscles clenching involuntarily. Then, the feeling let up for a few moments, and a feeling like, but not quite the same as relaxation flowed through her body.

"Do not panic, but... I think I saw something pressing from within you," Adam remarked.

"What! Did you think it, or did you see it? Tell me what happened."

"I think that I saw it!"

"Which one was it, Adam! Look closer!" Nova directed with a sternness in her voice that shocked Adam as her hand drew Adam closer to her stomach.

"I do not see anything anymore," Adam replied, his voice trembling. "Do you feel anything?"

"Not at the moment," Nova replied as the two fell into a bout of silence. "Come closer and take a listen," Nova demanded, again pressing Adam's head to her belly. "Tell me what you hear."

"Oof!" Nova and Adam exclaimed in unison. "Something poked me!" Adam announced.

"Me too!" Nova announced.

"What could it be? What do we do? What is happening?" Adam rambled in a bout of panic.

"Let us calm ourselves, Adam."

"Calm? Did you consume a thing that moves? I thought we agreed to never consume a thing that moves. We are also things that move and do not ourselves wish to be consumed."

"No, Adam. I have not."

"Have you allowed those things you consume to pass through you?"

"Yes, always. It is not a matter of consumption, Adam."

Nova and Adam continued to explore the possibilities, each idea as fantastical or horrific as the next.

Meanwhile, the Chairman attentively monitored the developments and had already implemented a plan to resolve the conflict within their minds. The Chairman had been concerned from the moment of news of the pregnancy that Nova and Adam would unknowingly cause harm to the unborn humanoid. The Chairman's plan was intended to assuage that concern by using a theory of communication through passive suggestions he had developed while researching studies on cross-species communication.

"Adam!" Nova exclaimed with excitement and clarity. Adam gave Nova his undivided attention. "Do you recall when I told you about the bird?"

"Umm… yes, maybe," Adam replied with a noticeable lack

of confidence, knowing that Nova had probably told him at a time when he was distracted with other activities.

"The bird had an egg, and one day, a smaller bird came out of the egg," Nova reminded Adam.

"Where did the egg come from?" Adam asked, still confused. "Maybe the bird's stomach," Adam added as he began understanding Nova's logical reasoning.

"What if..." Nova paused to think to herself and search her reasoning again. "What if I can create a smaller me? What if I am creating a smaller me?"

Adam raised his hand to his head and began scratching as he thought about what Nova was suggesting. Adam then started gently poking Nova's midsection. "I do not feel an egg. The egg was hard, correct?"

"Remember when you knocked down a beehive, and it broke open?"

"Yes, that was very painful. Is that how you feel now?"

"No. Inside, I saw smaller bees. I did not see any eggs. Another me could be growing inside of me and might not need an egg. It will come out." Nova added.

"Hmm..." Adam thought about it for a moment. "I cannot say it is untrue," Adam replied. "How did the creatures grow other creatures? What happened after the creatures were created? When will it come out of you?" Adam propounded question after question. The constant questioning created a sense of irritation within Nova, which she had not experienced before, and a sense of appreciation for Adam's attentiveness and interest.

The two sat under the tree and sometimes walked around, engaged in conversation, throughout the remainder of the day as dusk came and went. Contractions came and went, increasing in frequency though the intensity had plateaued.

Viewers tuned in intently, eager to watch the humanoids expand their horizons and experience the creation of life for the first time. It was an utter spectacle, a worldwide event. In the comments on the stream, many viewers remarked that they had never thought about many of the questions being discussed by the humanoids. Some commenters even remarked on how logical the conversation between Nova and Adam had become and how rapidly their artificial intelligence had worked through the problems.

The ease with which the humanoids had reached conclusions that took human scholars centuries to understand caused a sense of unease among some viewers but a sense of hope among others. Until this point, AI and machine learning algorithms had not been used in such a real-life scenario but instead had been focused on relatively mundane tasks. Now, some worried that the AI would advance to the point of understanding fully what they were and what they were capable of.

A small but strong contingent of commenters expressed that these occurrences were further proof that PomenTech was immoral, while others remarked that the humanoids were amoral. Either way, the viewership and level of interaction with the Chairman's live stream was steadily the most watched stream in the world, or at least in the Chairman's world.

"I love you, Adam," Nova said in a gentle, sleepy tone as she rested her head on his shoulder, the sun setting in the background.

"I love you as well, Nova," Adam replied as he gently rubbed her stomach.

CHAPTER 21

Project Cloak and Dagger

Haida was asleep. The wretched sound of metal screeching against concrete startled her awake. She knew that sound. It was mealtime, and a metal food tray had been, yet again, carelessly slid across the floor towards her by some mysterious figure.

The cell swallowed Haida in dimness, where even the rays of light fought to sneak through the narrow slit of a window. The metallic screech of the food tray against the concrete floor echoed off the walls like a reminder of her captivity.

The window was too narrow for a human body to fit through, but Haida had fantasized about how she could squeeze her already narrow frame through it and escape to the glorious freedom she had always enjoyed. She knew that if only a few slithers of light could make the squeeze, she had no chance. Nonetheless, she dreamed on, passing the time.

In the silence of her confinement, Haida clung to her dreams of escape, replaying them like her favorite nostalgic tv show. She could almost feel Mexico's arms around her, smell the familiar cologne he wore, and hear his voice promising to find her, to save her. She dreamt of him commanding every resource at his call to scour the earth for the love of his life. She dreamt of him quickly discovering whoever had the audacity to accost her in this fashion and dealing out the type of swift justice that comes from harming a powerful man's wife. She dreamt of her

Mexico rolling up his sleeves, bursting into her prison, wielding nothing but his bare hands and broad shoulders, and carrying her away. But reality slammed into her like a cold wave each time she opened her eyes.

There was no glass on the window, just two metal bars. Haida used all her willpower to rise to her feet and reach the window. The sun's warmth on her cheek was a distant memory, a brief reprieve from the cold dampness that clung to her skin like a second layer. For a moment, she forgot about her troubles, her prison, her lack of bathing, and the gastronomic disaster of a meal bubbling on the other side of the room.

Haida was so shocked by the amenities of this new location that she had not initially noticed the towering skyscrapers of downtown Chicago adorning the view from her prison. Indeed, she had not initially noticed that she was now in an actual jail cell teetering in the skyline. Still, she could not help but notice that the world outside had moved on without her. The city's distant hum seeped through the cracks of the walls, an ever-present reminder of freedom just beyond her reach.

"Hello?" Haida's voice cracked against the walls. "Water. Please," she added with a forced, mocking politeness, knowing too well it would fall on deaf ears. After a few moments, a reused bottle of water was tossed into her cell. The bottle had no label, was crinkled as if it had been squeezed more than a few times, and the water inside had a slight gray tint. Haida grabbed the bottle and immediately dropped it.

"Ouch!" Haida shrieked. "You jerks! You absolute clowns! Why would you give me a steaming hot bottle of water?" Haida yelled out as she held back tears.

Haida gently grabbed the water bottle, wrapping a piece of fabric around it. She placed it on the window to allow it to cool down. She then skeptically approached the food tray and slowly took in a spoonful of the nondescript oatmeal-like food in the tray lying on the floor.

"One day, I'm gonna get out of here, and you'll wish you were decent humans to me," Haida said under her breath, hoping her captors heard her just enough to think they knew what she said but not enough to be certain enough to retaliate against her. "I've never hurt anyone, but I'm gonna hurt you bad, so bad," Haida continued.

Haida had grown accustomed to talking to herself. It was her odd way of maintaining sanity. Her conversations ranged from gripes about her current situation and fantasizing about escaping to discussions of the meaning of life and whether life was just one big messed-up simulation run by an inhumane and/or incompetent operator. In a strange way, she felt a small amount of appreciation for her situation in that it had allowed her to take a step back from the rat race of life and think about what her true purpose was.

In her time, she had concluded that she was a miniscule piece of an infinitely massive ecosystem. In her quest to find the meaning of her life, Haida posited to herself a simple yet profound question, *"Does a mosquito question its purpose?"*

Naturally, she would play her role just by existing, she posited to herself. For example, simply breathing helped convert oxygen to carbon dioxide, which the earth used to keep itself warm and plants used as a part of the photosynthesis process, she told herself. Her job, she determined, was simply to live her life with as much enjoyment as possible while simultaneously creating the least amount of unenjoyment for others and avoiding negating the positive impact of her positive existence.

Shortly after placing the bottle of hot water on the window ledge, Haida heard a phone ring in the distance. No one answered, but she could hear the distinct sound of her captors shuffling around in a somewhat sporadic state. The phone began to ring again. Then, she heard a deep, yet womanly, voice answer the call. Haida was certain her senses had gotten better during her captivity. She listened closely.

"Are you finally ready to play ball?" the voice asked. Haida could not hear the person who called. "Good. We're glad you came to your senses," the voice continued. "Your precious girlfriend is safe and sound." In an instant, Haida's heart began to beat faster. "You'll receive the details shortly. Follow the instructions strictly, and all will be swell," the voice directed before abruptly ending the call.

"Yes, it's happening!" Haida exclaimed quietly to herself as she bounced up and down as discreetly as she could. A slew of commotion began outside of her cell and down a hall where she could not see. The sound of chairs sliding and objects being moved and perhaps packed up at a rapid pace simultaneously caused Haida excitement and anxiety.

"The stream is down!" a young man's voice yelled out from down the hall.

"Get me verification from our internal asset," the same woman's voice demanded.

After a few moments of silence passed, the young man's voice exclaimed, "Confirmed! Our asset confirms that the Genesis Box has been shut down."

"Permanently?" the woman's voice asked.

"Affirmative, permanently! Decommissioned!" the young man replied as cheers erupted within the prison's halls.

Haida was confused as to how many individuals were involved, whether that was the kidnappers' sole request, and who the internal asset was. Nonetheless, she brushed off those thoughts for another day, eager for her rescue.

Through the window's narrow slit, Haida heard the distant rumble of engines—"*a transport vehicle, perhaps?*" she thought to herself. Her pulse quickened. "*Could they be here for me—to finally rescue me? Or is this just another false hope to dangle my freedom just out of reach?*"

Then, the door creaked open with a low, ominous groan, sending a jolt of fear down Haida's spine. Two shadowy figures slipped into the room, their faces hidden behind black ski masks, making their eyes appear cold and hollow. Without a word, they grabbed her roughly by the arms, the coarse fabric of their gloves scraping against her skin. Before she could react, a blindfold was yanked over her eyes, plunging her into total darkness. They escorted her out of the cell, through a series of doors, and down what seemed to Haida like a maze of hallways and corridors.

With the blindfold squeezing painfully against her eyelids, Haida could only hear the muffled footsteps of her captors as they led her down a series of hallways. Every step echoed in the eerie silence, amplifying her disorientation. The sound of doors creaking open, the whirr of machinery, and the sudden drop in temperature made her suspect she had been placed in an elevator. Still, without sight, every sound felt distorted, every shift in motion unsettling.

She was then exited from the building, the distinct feel of the air surrounding her body and slight glimmers of sunlight piercing through the blindfold. She was placed into the back of a vehicle. A seatbelt was placed around her, and she was buckled into place, a measure she found to be ironic given how this all started. Haida could hear others getting into other vehicles as well, but she could not determine how many people or vehicles were in the convoy. The vehicles then departed.

There was a loud commotion as Haida's vehicle entered what sounded like motorized gates.

"Why has the gate closed?" the driver asked.

"I'm not sure. I didn't do anything," the individual in the passenger seat replied.

"Just get it open so we can be on our way," the driver demanded.

"It's not…" At that moment, there were a series of bright flashes of lights burst through the fabric of Haida's blindfold, followed immediately by a series of deafening bangs. Haida ducked instinctively, her heart hammering in her chest. Managing to remove the blindfold, she peeked out the window to see that the vehicle in which she was being transported had been trapped between an inner prison gate and an outer prison gate.

Despite the commotion around her, a sense of calm flowed across her body and mind. Through thick clouds of smoke, Haida could see smoke emanating from canisters on the ground. She noticed the smoke parting ways as if someone was walking through the smoke. She recalled her dreams of Mexico saving her in a heroic fashion.

She waited but saw no one walking through the smoke. No slow motion, steamy reveal of a heroic figure to whisk her away. Then, in an instant, the two front doors of the vehicle were thrown open, and the driver and passenger were removed from the vehicle with sudden and extreme force and knocked unconscious. Still, Haida could not see anyone.

Then, the gate opened, the vehicle doors closed, and the car began to drive forward. The sense of calm Haida experienced immediately drained from her body and mind and she felt a pit in her stomach like she was in freefall on a rollercoaster. She let out a scream and reached to open the door but could not because her hands were still bound. Amid the thick, swirling smoke, a calm voice broke through the chaos, soft yet authoritative.

"Ma'am, please remain calm. The Chairman sent us." Haida's breath hitched in her throat, her mind struggling to grasp the sudden shift from terror to relief.

Then, like magic, two individuals appeared in front of her. One in the driver's seat and the other in the passenger seat. Dressed in seamless gray suits that clung to their bodies like a second skin, the individuals seemed to shimmer as they moved.

The fabric was unlike anything Haida had ever seen—smooth, metallic, and almost liquid in how it shifted under the light. Their faces were obscured by sleek, featureless helmets, making them appear more machine than human. "The Chairman has been working on this new technology," one of them said, their voice distorted slightly by a hidden microphone, adding to the sense of unreality. "It was originally meant for government use, but the Chairman recently decided to end PomenTech's government contract, whether the government knows it yet or not."

Haida was at a loss for words.

"We have been tracking the locations of the insurgents. The Chairman's algorithm helped us get one step ahead of them. We knew they would take you to the Cook County Jail, and we planned this rescue."

Haida remained silent—shocked.

The rescuers asked Haida if she had any injuries and continued to try to assuage her concerns. The car stopped after what felt like the longest ride of Haida's existence. The restraints were removed from her, and she was helped out of the vehicle. She was at the Tower of Innovation.

Haida fully expected to be whisked up the elevator to see the Chairman standing in his high tower, cloaked in the safety and luxury of his surroundings, weeping over his precious Genesis Box. As she expected, the driver escorted Haida to the Chairman's private elevator. As the elevator doors closed, the driver removed his mask.

"Mexico!" Haida exclaimed.

The Chairman opened his mouth, but no words came out. Instead, the two looked deeply at each other and shared a long embrace, gentle tears of joy and pain building up in their eyes. Their bodies were both trembling, and they were each surprised to witness the other in such a raw emotional state. They bonded more than ever.

Sophie promptly greeted the two as they exited the elevator. She embraced them both like a child longing for and excited for her parents' return. Sophie whisked the two away as she prepared a warm bath with calming scents, relaxing music, and their favorite teas.

Later, as Mexico and Haida sat on the couch overlooking the setting sun, he explained to Haida how he had duped the kidnappers into believing his Genesis Box had been shut down to encourage them to drop their guard. That momentary lapse in judgment, he explained, was just enough to allow the rescue plan to proceed successfully. He hoped to share that information to passively admit to Haida that he did not shut down his Genesis Box.

"That was very brave and unexpected of you," Haida said. "And I'm happy you decided to not to destroy your Genesis World."

"Yeah, since I created it, I have a responsibility to protect it," Mexico replied reflectively. "But, unexpected?" he questioned while laughing. "I'm appalled that you think so little of me. I'm very heroic."

"You know what I mean," Haida responded, lovingly caressing his face. "I'm just glad you didn't get hurt. You're a real-life action hero. My hero."

Mexico wrapped his arm around Haida's shoulder and pulled her closer as the sun was almost gone. Haida squeezed in closer to him as the two cuddled.

"You know you're not gonna get off that easily," she said jokingly. "You mean to tell me this could've all been ended if you just shut down the Genesis Box?" she continued.

Mexico looked into the distance as his chest tightened. He could manage no words in that moment. After forcing him to struggle for a few moments, Haida responded. "You know I fully understand, right?"

"You do?" the Chairman replied.

"Yeah, I understand the duality of the importance of your greatest creation and your greatest love," she said while smiling. "I understand the impact Genesis can have on the world and its understanding of life. Not just life as we know it but life beyond our preconceived definition."

Mexico nodded his head in agreement. "I've never really said this aloud," he added. "But, Nova and Adam could very well be just as real... just as human as you and I." A heavy pause filled the air before as Haida nodded in silent agreement. He continued, "I mean... who's to say we aren't living in our very own Genesis World?"

The two stared at eachother for a moment and then let out a nervous laugh.

CHAPTER 22

The Introduction

Mexico was gently awakened by the warmth of the sun's rays. His very first thought of the day was Haida Markle. *"Had it all been just a dream*," he thought to himself in a small panic. He rolled over calmly and confirmed that his dreams were now his reality. Haida sat propped against a stack of pillows, the early sunlight casting a warm glow on her, surprising still perfect skin.

Haida's fingers traced the edges of a worn novel, her expression serene as she lost herself in its pages. She responded to Mexico's gaze with a warm smile. As he met her warm smile, a quiet relief washed over him, dispelling the unease that had lingered from the night before. He felt more connected to her than ever, grateful for their shared understanding.

"What are you reading?" Mexico whispered.

"We are God," Haida whispered back. "Have you read it before?"

"No. What is it about, if you don't mind me asking," Mexico responded as he tried in vain not to get lost in her eyes.

"Come have morning tea with me, and I'll give you the synopsis. It's right up your alley."

"I would love to," he replied. "But first, I need to say something," he added.

Haida's gaze shifted from her novel to Mexico's eyes. With a cute and vulnerable nervousness, he dropped to one knee, grabbed Haida's hand and spoke from his heart. "Haida, I have loved you from the day we met. Really, before you even knew who I was. Of course, you are the most beautiful woman I have ever seen. But there is so much more to you. Your energy is intoxicating. I love just being with you. And that's it, when I'm with you, I can just be me." The Chairman continued as Haida smiled lovingly, a few tears of joy drifting down her rosy cheeks. "Haida Markle, I love you and want to spend the rest of my life with you. Will you do me the honor of marrying me?"

"Yes. Yes. Yes!" Haida replied, now crying uncontrollably, as the two rose to their feet, hugging one another as if never to let go.

Sophie entered the room as Mexico and Haida sat having tea on the terrace overlooking the city that had once held them captive, but had also given them what they valued most in life.

"Good morning, love birds!" Sophie stated with excitement. "Terrance is here to see you."

"Thank you, Sophie. But, if it isn't urgent, I will speak with him later," Mexico replied.

"He's here to speak with aunty Haida. I think he has just a few questions," Sophie replied. Haida and Sophie shared a glance and a chuckle.

"Sure thing. You can send him in," Haida replied.

Terrance was visibly taken aback to see the Chairman in pajamas, and no less, with a woman by his side. The Chairman had always presented a polished and clean look. Terrance immediately composed himself.

"Good morning, sir. Ma'am, I require just a moment of your time," Terrance stated formally.

"Certainly, Terrance. What do you need?" Haida replied.

"Ma'am," Terrance began, his voice low and steady, "we'll go over everything later, but for now, I need to ask—during your ordeal, did you ever hear the name MJ?" His words hung in the air, heavy and loaded with meaning.

"Umm… No. I can't say that I have," Haida replied.

"Janina?" The sunlight that had seemed so welcoming earlier now felt harsh, casting sharp shadows across the room. The peaceful morning air was thick with unspoken questions as Terrance stood, waiting for Haida's answer.

"Nope. I never heard them speaking much. It was weird."

"What is this about, Terrance?" Mexico interjected.

"Sir, the individual we had arrested on suspicion of the attack on your system was one MJ, a PomenTech employee," Terrance replied.

"Did she have something to do with the kidnapping?" Mexico asked, a look of perplexion and disbelief written on his face.

"We have no information that would support that, sir. We are just trying to cover all bases and close the investigation."

"I would like to speak with her. Will you set up a VR meeting?"

"Sir, we have her in the building now for questioning. Would you like to join me?"

Without hesitation, Mexico replied, "Yes, I will be ready momentarily."

"Certainly, sir. I will wait for you outside."

Mexico began getting dressed. Haida began getting dressed too.

"You know I'm going with you, right?" Haida stated.

"Are you looking for a scoop or just don't want to leave my side," the Chairman joked.

"The latter sounds better. Jokes aside, I won't write about any of this if you don't want me to. The kidnapping, the hacking, any of it. Just let me know what you want. Believe me, I am perfectly happy if we never have to speak of this again."

"No," Mexico replied in a reassuring voice. "I would never ask you to keep something like this to yourself. I know how much investigative journalism means to you, and it doesn't get more investigative than being locked in a jail cell as a captive of some idealist nutjobs."

"I'm not sure they were completely nutty, but we'll save that for a later discussion," Haida replied, half joking. "Let's get moving to talk to this MJ. For some reason, she sounds like she would be good at basketball."

As Mexico opened the double doors leading from his office into the lobby area on his floor, his face changed from joyful to stern. Led by Terrance in front, Sophie on his right, and Haida on his left, Mexico entered the elevator and descended to the sublevel where MJ was being held.

The group entered the security office, where they could see MJ sitting in a chair at a table in a room with one light directly above her, beaming down with such intensity that she had begun to perspire. However, MJ could not see them as they were hidden behind a soundproof two-way mirror. After a moment to compose himself, Mexico decided to enter the room. Terrance followed behind him, while Sophie and Haida remained behind the glass.

"Ma'am, thank you for your patience," Terrance told MJ.

"Sure," MJ replied, her voice quivering. She spoke to Terrance, but her eyes were on Mexico as if he was a father she had tragically disappointed.

"The officers have explained to you that you are being charged with unlawful computer access and assorted related crimes, do you understand that?" Terrance said, his voice stern and unyielding.

"Yes," MJ replied, her voice meek and apologetic.

"Yes and?" Terrance asked as he stared at MJ and deliberately allowed a pregnant pause to smother the room.

"Like I said to the officer, I'm sorry," MJ replied.

Terrance allowed another pregnant pause to fill the room like lung-choking smoke. Mexico stood in silence in a corner, his arms crossed and his legs in a wide, athletic stance.

"Sorry for what?" Mexico chimed in from the corner with an angry tone that matched that of a disappointed father.

"For everything. You all aren't cops, are you? Well, I know you are not Mr. Chairman," MJ remarked.

"No," Terrance responded. "I'm just a security officer who works for PomenTech."

MJ picked up on Terrance's slight lie, sparking further suspicion within her. "And you're not recording me, are you?" MJ asked.

Terrance walked to the corner of the room where Mexico was standing. "Sir, may I?" Terrance asked as he reached up behind Mexico and disconnected a few wires. "No, we are not recording you," Terrance replied to MJ.

Mexico moved away from the corner, and his face was now fully visible to MJ. The two shared a glance, almost as if they could read each other's minds. "Terrance, will you please give me and MJ a moment?" Mexico said.

Terrance reluctantly agreed and left the room, the weight of his combat boots drifting into the distance, lightening the mood with each step away.

"Okay. Talk to me," Mexico stated to MJ as he got down on one knee to have a more connected conversation with her.

"What do you want me to say?" MJ replied.

"The truth. And start from the beginning. I want to know who you really are, how you got to this moment, and why?"

MJ let out a sigh. Not a sigh of annoyance, but a sigh as if she were releasing a burden from her mind. "My name is Michelle James, but everyone calls me MJ."

"I know that much," Mexico interrupted. "I know you were a Junior Developer and transitioned to Marketing, where you showed substantial promise and were on the path to leadership."

MJ was pleasantly surprised. She felt seen.

"But if we're being formal, my name is Jay Moor but you can call me Mr. Chairman," Mexico responded with a bit of levity. "Now that we have formalities out of the way, how did we get to this point?" Mexico said.

MJ walked through her life story, from her dreams to meeting George and being betrayed by George. She talked to about how she felt cheated and stolen from. She expressed her strong connection to the Genesis World and felt like it was her baby, her grand creation. She explained that she always knew it would be a massive team effort but never expected to be so left out and receive zero credit.

"MJ, I knew all about George and his alleged theft. And I'm sure it was true," Mexico replied, as a look of shock plastered across MJ's face. "I was not going to let him get away with it," Mexico continued. "At the same time, we did not need any scandals, media attention, or anything abnormal surrounding this project. Do you understand?"

"Not completely," MJ muttered.

"Still, I recognize that I should have taken action earlier," Mexico continued. "For that, I apologize."

Tears began to form in MJ's eyes.

"You do realize we never announced any tangible prize for the Innovation Competition, right?" Mexico said.

"I guess...I guess not," MJ replied as she tried to keep herself from crying."

"Seriously, I was going to make sure you were taken care of... just in due time, my friend," Mexico added. "After all, you don't get as big as PomenTech by failing to care for your stars—both risen and rising."

His words brought an intense sense of relief to MJ along with a sense that she was finally seen. The rush of emotions she felt at that moment quietly burst to the surface as her eyes began to water over, and tears began silently pouring from her eyes.

As the conversation continued, Mexico's eyes were opened to how MJ had perceived him treating her and disregarding her ideas without a second thought. He had reasons for his action and did not agree with her interpretation, but he did not wish to take up that moment by throwing excuses and micro invalidations at MJ. Instead, he sat and conversed with her for as long as she wanted to talk. He felt a strange sense of connection to MJ.

When MJ had gotten her story out, Mexico explained that her actions had caused unintended consequences greater in value than anything he had imagined. He explained that the success of the Genesis Box was not fully in traditional sales but instead mostly in viewership, the insight it provided into human development and the ecosystem, and other areas he could not discuss with her. She knew what he meant.

Mexico's Genesis Box had garnered millions of views each day since the awakening of the humanoids. The result was the equivalent of having a sports championship game streamed live every day. For that, he thanked MJ sincerely.

"Sir, I have to say that I am truly shocked," MJ stated. "I for sure thought you were going to be peeved and throw me in a corporate dungeon somewhere. Or worse… into that god-awful fireplace in the boardroom."

"I mean… you're not off of the hook," Mexico responded as he rose from his chair and left MJ alone in the room.

"Terrance, what will happen to this young woman?" Mexico asked as he entered the security office where Terrance, Sophie, and Haida were waiting.

"Well, sir. Criminal charges are pending against her. I will have to confirm with counsel, but I do believe you have the right to request withdrawal of those charges because she has not yet had her formal arraignment date," Terrance replied.

Mexico glanced at Sophie and Haida. They both gave him the same look as if to tell him that he knew what to do. Mexico thought for a moment and then asked the others to give him a moment alone so he could think more. Alone in the security office, he paced back and forth in the small space, speaking to himself.

"*What message would we be sending if we let a hacker off the hook? I have a zero-tolerance policy and cannot make exceptions for anyone without looking out of control. How can we punish her without ruining her future? What if this becomes catastrophic? What if the effects of the virus are not done? What if she made this whole story up to get sympathy?"* Mexico's thoughts were wild but controlled.

He then invited the group back into the security office. He looked at Haida and Sophie again, and they gave him the same look again. He sighed the same sigh MJ had released earlier. Then, he returned to the room with MJ as Haida and Sophie watched, and Terrance followed.

"Tell me this. Do you know whether this virus is done changing our programming?" Mexico asked.

"I can't say. Like I said, I didn't know it would even go this far. That's the nature of it," MJ replied.

"Tell me this. Do you enjoy being in marketing?"

"Yes, I guess."

"You guess? Do you enjoy it as much as being on the development team?"

"No, sir. Of course not."

Mexico stood in silence for a moment. "Here's what I am going to do. You are going to be my lead on Project Compass."

"Project Compass?"

"Yes. You will develop and refine a robust behavioral code for the humanoids that instills what are essentially morals and values. The goal is to build the proper structure for creating a Genesis Society that values life, freedom, and equality – things we seem to have failed at in this world. We've already gotten started, but it is far from where it needs to be. Does that make sense?"

MJ took a moment to consider what Mexico was saying. "Yes, yes, that makes perfect sense, and I agree completely." MJ began to mumble to herself about what tasks she would need to complete and how to get them to work.

"Your buddy... Janina. I want you to recruit her to be my cybersecurity consultant. Got it?"

"Janina is... she's not the corporate type, you know?"

"You're in leadership at PomenTech now. You know what that means?"

"Umm... I"

"That means you need to figure out how to make the impossible possible," Mexico interrupted her. "I give you a task; you find a way to get it done. Understood?"

"Understood, sir. What about the criminal charges?"

"How about twenty years of hyper-speed simulated prison, which would only take about a week in the real world?"

MJ froze, and the room went silent. "I'm just kidding, everyone! Sheesh! You all are too uptight" Mexico interjected as he let out a robust laugh. "A jail cell rarely cultivates greatness. And trust me, MJ. There is greatness within you."

CHAPTER 23

New Growth

The artificiality of life made it no less valuable.

Nova sat in the soft green grass, her fingers sinking into the damp blades cool against her skin. She leaned back, her palms pressed into the earth, feeling the subtle contours of the ground beneath as if the world itself was breathing. Adam clutched her hand with his. With her feet flat on the ground, knees raised, and legs spread, Nova instinctively began to push.

Screaming helped. Squeezing Adam's hand helped. Biting her tongue did not help, but the salty taste of blood and minor pain in comparison to the excruciating pain with which she was dealing provided a welcome reprieve. She wanted it all to end.

No matter how bad the feeling was, however, Nova did her best to remain focused on her critical role in the world. She was bringing about life itself. Surely, she could endure for such a grand purpose. *"There is a baby relying on you,"* she thought to herself repeatedly. *"You can do this."*

The ordeal had begun hours ago. Adam was also ready for it to end, but he kept the feeling to himself. Instead, he peppered Nova with words intended to encourage. Adam, however, was lost and unsure what would happen. Then it happened.

"It's coming out!" Nova exclaimed as she writhed. "Look and see! I can feel it!"

Adam slowly left Nova's side and crept toward her legs. "I see something," Adam replied. He waited for a moment. "Push just a little more," Adam remarked.

Nova pushed again. "A head! I see a head!" Adam yelled. "Keep going, my love!"

Nova mustered all the might she could manage and pushed again. This push was more robust than the others, emanating from deep within her as if she was drawing strength from the millions of viewers she had no clue existed.

"Shoulders! I see shoulders!" Adam yelled.

"Get it out of me!" Nova screamed.

Adam collected himself. He reached to grab the shoulders. Just as he got close enough to touch the shoulders, Nova pushed again, and the baby humanoid gently fell into Adam's hands.

Nova let out a sigh of relief. A silence fell over the space. The baby was not moving. Nova was not moving. Silence filled the air.

Then, in an instant, the baby let out a short, shallow cry. Nova smiled. Adam looked concerned and relieved, all at the same time.

Adam inspected the newborn from head to toe. He noted that the baby had male genitalia like him and was still physically attached to Nova. Nova, breathing heavily, stretched out her arms toward the baby.

"Here. Take a look," Adam stated as he handed the baby to Nova. "He is beautiful," Adam remarked.

Exhausted, Nova did not look at the baby but instead held him gently against her chest, content with feeling his presence. The baby became calm and stopped crying. Nova then fell asleep, baby in her arms with Adam watching over them.

Nova and Adam named the child Michael Ibere James, Ibere for short. Their love for Ibere and shared purpose in life brought Adam and Nova closer, both as a family and romantically. Ibere lived an enjoyable life, nurtured by his parents but allowed to roam free and explore. In those days, danger was limited.

Nova would go on to birth more children, six boys and six girls, in total. The children of Nova inherited code from their parents, including the corrupted code. And so, the cycle began and continued.

Nova became pregnant for the thirteenth time around her 902,280th tick, which equates to 103 human years. Nova's body had degraded from physical stress and was no longer able to operate effectively. Neither she nor the unborn humanoid survived the pregnancy.

Because her memory system was biotech, her memories decayed into minor electric energy that dissipated into the Genesis World. Parts of her code, however, lived on in her offspring.

Adam had preceded Nova in death during his 814,680th tick. Nova was by his side as his body shut down.

"I am incredibly proud to have journeyed with you," Nova said as she had held Adam's hand. Adam managed a smile, which gave Nova joy to witness one last time. Adam did not speak. Instead, the two stared into each other, savoring the moment for an eternity. Then it was over.

After Adam's death, Nova had continued to live her life, watching as the population of humanoids to which she was mother grew exponentially. Nova watched as a society developed, advancements were made, and failures led to new innovations. Nova watched as generations beget generations.

After Nova's death, generations continued to beget generations, and the population of the Genesis World grew with each tick, growing closer and closer to Mexico's prediction of overpopulation.

Meanwhile, despite Mexico's initial goal of being highly involved in crafting his Genesis World, he became less and less involved over time. Life, wife, and kids had become more important to him. Still, he was comfortable knowing that he had created the proper base for the Genesis Society to thrive.

Without substantial oversight from Mexico, his Genesis World took on a life of its own. MJ had implemented a moral code in the early stages of the Genesis Society's formation. However, updates stopped after Mexico resigned from his position as Chairman and CEO.

The U.S. government had not been pleased with Mexico's decision to withdraw from Strategy Nine and all government contracts. In response, government actors intentionally brought about a series of events that threatened a hostile takeover of PomenTech.

Mexico, armed with the best corporate lawyers in the world and nearly unlimited financial resources, could have mounted a strong fight against the takeover. Instead, however, he voluntarily gave up his positions, content with spending his remaining time on earth with his family, pursuing his passions, and using his financial and political power to help make his world a better place.

Still, the Genesis Box remained powered on. Following a contentious court battle, an order was issued requiring the Genesis Box to remain powered on as long as life existed within. Thus, the Genesis World continued, tucked away in some corner of the Tower of Innovation.

Mexico's Genesis Box became little more than an inconsequential line item on the company's financial statements, evoking nostalgia when casually discussed. To the humanoids, however, it was their entire world.

A vestige of a relic, the Genesis World was left to its own eventual destruction. Overpopulation was the cause, war was the effect, and artificial intelligence was the tool.

THE END

ABOUT THE AUTHOR

E.d. Moore

E.D. Moore is an author and attorney passionate about storytelling that challenges the boundaries of imagination and reality. Drawing on his professional expertise and creative vision, Moore crafts narratives that explore human ambition, ethical dilemmas, and the interplay between technology and society in action-packed scenarios.

A corporate espionage attorney, Moore spends his days advising companies on complex legal issues and his nights diving into the depths of speculative fiction. His unique perspective and meticulous attention to detail allow him to build intricate worlds while grounding them in universally resonating themes.

When not writing or practicing law, Moore enjoys exploring apocalyptic films, late 90s and early 2000s music, running, traveling, and spending time with his family. Project Genesis: The Genesis Paradox is his debut novel, thrillingly exploring the blurred lines between artificial intelligence and humanity.

For updates on upcoming projects or to connect with the author, visit www.pomenishi.com

www.ingramcontent.com/pod-product-compliance
Lightning Source LLC
Chambersburg PA
CBHW031604260626

47154CB00020B/1296